THE BOY WHO MADE MONSTERS

JENNY PEARSON

ILLUSTRATED BY KATIE KEAR

USBORNE

For Rebecca Hill,
this book was always for you

First published in the UK in 2023 by Usborne Publishing Limited,
Usborne House, 83-85 Saffron Hill, London EC1N 8RT, England. usborne.com

Usborne Verlag, Usborne Publishing Limited, Prüfeninger St 20, 93049
Regensburg, Deutschland, VK Nr. 17560

Text © Jenny Pearson, 2023.

The right of Jenny Pearson to be identified as the author of this work has been
asserted by her in accordance with the Copyright, Designs and Patents Act, 1988.

Cover and inside illustrations by Katie Kear © Usborne Publishing, 2023.

Title typography by Thy Bui © Usborne Publishing, 2023.
Author name typography by Sarah Coleman © Usborne Publishing, 2023.

The name Usborne and the Balloon logo are Trade Marks of
Usborne Publishing Limited.

A CIP catalogue record for this book is available from the British Library.

ISBN 9781474999892 7494/1 JFMA JJASOND/23

Printed and bound using 100% renewable energy at CPI Group (UK) Ltd,
Croydon, CR0 4YY.

MIX
Paper | Supporting
responsible forestry
FSC® C171272

THE THING ABOUT MONSTERS

The first thing you need to know about monsters is they're real. I understand if you find that hard to believe. My big brother Stanley thinks you shouldn't believe *anything* you're told, unless you have weighed up all the evidence. He's a bit of a joy-sucker like that. Always questioning, never just believing.

But sometimes there isn't any evidence. Sometimes, you need to have the vision to believe that the most unlikely things can happen. Like a monster living at the bottom of a loch. Or that your parents will come home safe, even when they've been missing for months.

Sometimes all you have to go on is a feeling.

I'm okay with trusting my feelings, because I am an incredibly visionary person – I have a lot of faith in feelings. But to be honest, I think most people are more like Stanley. They want cold hard proof before they'll believe something. For instance, when you say, "I saw a monster in the loch with my very own eyeballs," people don't say, "Wow, that's amazing! How big was it?" They say, "There must be something very wrong with your eyeballs," or they say, "You, Benji McLaughlin, have lost your conkers. Where's your proof?"

This leads me on to the second thing you need to know about monsters. They like to go about their monstering unnoticed, which is a bit inconvenient. Loch monsters in particular don't like having their photo taken. They lurk under the surface – there but not always seen. This is very annoying when you're trying to prove to people that they exist, and this is the reason why my friend Murdy Mei-Yin McGurdy and I ended up having to create our own evidence to convince people that the Loch Lochy Monster was a real-life,

living, breathing thing. You might think this is a bit of a dishonest move on our parts, and maybe you're right, but it was for a very good cause.

It was for Uncle Hamish.

And the third thing you need to know about monsters is this: there are a lot of different types of monster. Some live at the bottom of lochs, some are found far out at sea and some swim about in the depths of your mind – if you let them – and these can be the scariest monsters of all. Some monsters could be considered bad, but some monsters turn out to be the exact opposite. Some monsters can bring out the best in people. Some monsters can challenge you to face your fears and make you see the truth.

This is a story about the Loch Lochy Monster and how, in some ways, it saved me. How it saved us all. And that's because it helped us to see what was really there and taught us to live with what we'd lost.

CHAPTER 1

A TRAIN TO THE START

Some stories start by telling you *exactly* what happened. Like in *James and the Giant Peach* when you find out James's parents were eaten by a rhinoceros that had escaped from the zoo. BAM. Just like that. Gobbled, gone, get over it.

But I can't do that. I don't want to talk about what happened. How our parents went missing at sea. How that shouldn't have happened when they were accomplished sailors.

What I'm going to do is start my story at a good place. And I guess the start of things getting better for me and Stanley was when we were sent up to Scotland to stay with our Uncle Hamish. It had taken a while. We'd been placed with a very lovely foster family, the Wests, while we were waiting for the news that we could stay with Uncle Hamish. Apparently, he had to jump through all sorts of hoops so the people in charge, social services I guess, would let us go and stay with him. The courts had to be very sure that he was the right person to look after us because he lived so far away, and we didn't know him *that* well.

Stanley was NOT happy about it at the time; he didn't want to leave London. I was okay with it. London didn't feel like home without Mum and Dad. Stanley had quite a strop about it but back then, Stanley was miserable about everything. Don't hold that against him – he was having a tough time. I suppose we both were. But on top of everything, Stanley had also turned thirteen. Dad had always warned me about the "transformation" – that as soon as a kid becomes a teenager, they go all moody and start grunting instead of talking. Which was *exactly* what happened to Stanley! I'm ten and a bit, so I've still got a couple of years until it happens to me. Although, I just can't see me changing like that. I like talking too much.

Uncle Hamish met us at Edinburgh train station in his beat-up old Land Rover. It seemed like ages since he'd first rushed down to London. That meeting was a bit of a blur. I can remember our social services lady, Maria, and Uncle Hamish and the bright red beanbags we all sat on. But I don't remember what was said. We'd seen him a few times after that, but always with someone official in the room, checking that everything was going okay.

I spotted him first, standing the other side of the barriers. I remember exactly what he was wearing – a pair of cargo shorts and a very-not-white T-shirt that looked like it had muddy paw prints on the front. Over the top, despite it being the summer, he had chosen to wear a blazer. It was like he'd remembered last minute that he should make an effort and grabbed the first thing he could to smarten himself up.

"What is he wearing?" Stanley said, clearly not impressed.

As the train pulled away behind us, I gripped hold of my suitcase handle tighter and whispered, "He really does look so much like Dad. Well, a taller, lingier version of Dad." I couldn't tear my eyes from his face, even though it kind of hurt to look at him.

I think Stanley must have felt weird about seeing Dad's almost-face again too, because he snapped at me. "There's no such word as lingier."

"Longer and stringier, then."

He couldn't disagree with that. Uncle Hamish is possibly the tallest real-life man I've ever seen. Stanley reckons he's over six foot seven. I think if he had lived in America and not in a teeny village beside Loch Lochy, he would have been a basketball player and not run holiday home rentals. Although maybe not a very good basketball player because he is a bit on the clumsy side.

Maria, our lady from social services who had come with us in case we got lost (which would be a very hard thing to do on a train), said, "Are you ready, boys? I think that's your uncle over there."

Stanley said, "What choice do we have?" Which sounded a bit rude, but I knew what he meant. We didn't have any choice. Uncle Hamish was the only family we had left.

Maria tilted her head in that way people had started doing to us once they'd heard what had happened. "I know this is difficult, but I think it really is for the best. Honestly, people go to Loch Lochy for their holidays. I hear it's a beautiful place. And your Uncle Hamish is very excited about having you to stay with him."

"He doesn't look excited. He looks like he doesn't

want to be here," Stanley muttered. Then even more quietly, so only I could hear, he said, "I don't want to be here."

I looked at Uncle Hamish. Stanley was right, he didn't seem *that* excited. He had his hands stuffed in his pockets and he was chewing his lip. But I don't think he looked like he didn't want to be there. To me, he looked more nervous than anything else. And he must have wanted us – we'd heard him say it to Maria enough times for me to think so. Maybe Stanley had just been choosing not to listen.

Maria bleeped herself through the barriers and bounded towards him shouting, "Mr McLaughlin, Hamish, Hamish, coo-eee!" Everyone who was milling around the train station turned to look because Maria was very loud and very noticeable in her bright pink suit and pointy yellow heels.

Stanley and I started after her at a much slower pace. I saw Stanley look over his shoulder back at the train tracks, like he was considering doing a runner, so I helped him through the ticket gate with a friendly shove.

We stood a few steps behind Maria while she shook Uncle Hamish's massive hand like she wanted to rip his arm out of the socket.

"It's wonderful to see you again. I've been telling the boys how good it will be for them staying here with you in your lovely home by the loch," she was saying. "The boys have talked of nothing else the whole train journey."

"Is that so?" Uncle Hamish said. His voice was quite soft, and it made me feel a bit less nervous.

It wasn't true that *we* had talked of nothing else, but I didn't see any point in highlighting Maria's lie. *I* had asked her a lot of important questions about our move.

Like whether we'd have to go to school now we lived in Scotland and, if we did, would I have to learn the bagpipes and, if so, were they easier than the French horn, because I tried to learn that in Year 4 and discovered I wasn't very good at blowy instruments. And if in PE lessons we'd have to practise throwing those caber tree-trunk things instead of cricket balls, because that would be cool. I'd asked if they had proper food, like pizza and chips or if we'd have to eat haggis all the time, because Dad had told me *all* about what they put in that stuff, and I was NOT sure I liked the sound of it. Although I would probably try it because I think you should try everything once – you never know, it could be great! I'd also asked if we'd have to wear a kilt and whether it was true that we wouldn't be allowed to wear underpants underneath even if it was really cold. I'd also checked if Uncle Hamish belonged to a clan and, if so, did that mean we belonged to a clan and would we be asked to do clan-type things, like painting our faces blue and white and running around on hills shouting, because I could really see myself getting into all that!

But Stanley hadn't asked *anything*. Not a thing. He just had his head in a book which was called *Understanding Mechanics*. I don't think it was a very good book though because I flicked through when he went to have a pee and it didn't have one interview with a mechanic in it. I think if you're going to understand somebody, you should ask them questions. Not draw a load of wiggly lines on graphs. But who am I to say? Stanley is way cleverer than me.

"Yes," Maria continued. "They are very excited to find out what life is like at Loch Lochy. Isn't that right, boys?"

Stanley shrugged but I said, "Oh yes. There is so much I would like to know. But the first thing I want to talk to you about is the Scottish underpants situation."

"The *what*?" Uncle Hamish said.

"Do you wear underpants?" I said.

Stanley shook his head and Uncle Hamish looked at me very strangely then said, "Yes."

"Excellent," I said. What a relief.

Maria said, "Right, well, now that important detail has been cleared up, let's move on to logistics. Mr McLaughlin, I know you've been in frequent communicado with my colleague Sandra, who is your local social services contact. She's the person to check in with if you have any problems and I know she'll be popping by soon to check the boys are all settled. She will also organize for Stanley to continue with a counsellor."

Stanley groaned and rolled his eyes. Like I said, he didn't like talking. Especially not to counsellors.

Not like me. I'd talked to my counsellor, Marvin, a lot.

In fact, I'd done so brilliantly in the months since Mum and Dad disappeared that Marvin said it was up to me if I continued. It annoyed Stanley that he still had to go and I didn't. But he'd been there when it had happened, and I hadn't. Although, it turns out, I wasn't necessarily talking about the right things. I probably didn't speak the truth. I wasn't ready to. That happened much later.

Maria checked her watch. "Well, on that note, I need to get to my platform, or I'll miss the train back to London." She gave us both a quick hug, clutched her hand to her chest and said, "You'll be fine, I promise. I'll keep in touch through Sandra and we're both going to make sure you're supported as a family." And then she was off, her yellow heels click-clacking across the concrete.

"As a family?" Stanley said quietly. I knew what he meant. This wasn't how our family was supposed to be. I reached out and held on to the bottom of his jacket, just to know he was still there.

The three of us stood there for a while. It was the first ever time we'd been on our own together. Stanley was studying his shoelaces. I was still holding on to his

jacket, while staring at Uncle Hamish's face trying to work out which bits were Dad and which were him. And Uncle Hamish was glancing from me to Stanley with this strange look in his eyes that could have been happy, sad, worried or a mixture of all three.

Eventually, Uncle Hamish clapped his hands together, which made both me and Stanley jump, and said, "Right we'd best be off, then. It is a wee bit of a drive to the loch."

We headed out into the train-station car park and loaded our bags into the back of the Land Rover, which Uncle Hamish called his pride and joy. When he was

paying for the parking, I said to Stanley, "He really does seem okay, don't you think? I like him."

Stanley shrugged. "You like everybody. He could be a monster for all we know, Benji."

Uncle Hamish obviously wasn't a monster. And he definitely wasn't the monster that Stanley or I had to worry about.

CHAPTER 2

A RIDE IN THE SNORKELLING LAND ROVER WITH MR DOG

We weren't long into our *wee* journey before I had decided that I very much liked Uncle Hamish's Land Rover. He said it was a Defender and that made me feel safe, although I'm not sure what it was defending us from. It had roof bars and this long plastic pipe thing that Uncle Hamish said was a snorkel and helped the truck get through big puddles. I had never in all my years heard of a car with its own snorkel. I wondered if it was another Scottish thing.

Stanley sat in the front, because he's the oldest and apparently those are the rules. But I didn't mind because I got to sit in the back on a bench, not a proper seat, with Uncle Hamish's dog, Mr Dog.

"Why's he called Mr Dog?" I asked.

"Why do you think?" I saw Stanley roll his eyes in the rear-view mirror. "It's not because he's an armadillo, is it?"

Obviously, Mr Dog wasn't an armadillo but if he had been called Mr Armadillo that would at least be a bit interesting. To be honest, I think Mr Dog's name showed a startling lack of vision. "Is it because Scottish people aren't very good at naming things?"

"What do you mean?" Uncle Hamish asked.

"Mr Dog – it's hardly very imaginative, is it? A bit like calling your loch, **Loch Lochy**. It's like someone named all the lakes in Scotland but when they got to yours, they ran out of ideas and just went – *well it's quite lochy looking, let's go with that.*"

Uncle Hamish laughed a deep, deep laugh which filled the whole Land Rover. "Well maybe when you see it, you might be able to come up with a better alternative, hey, laddie?"

"Okay, I will," I said, because it would be easy to come up with a better name than Loch Lochy. "I'm sure

I can think of something visionary. Mum and Dad say I have a very good imagination."

"And I'm sure they are right about that. Your da—" Uncle Hamish suddenly stopped and did this little swallow like his words were struggling to get out of him. He did a few more swallows, then let out a long breath. "I really am sorry, boys – about what happened to your folks. A terrible thing..." Then he sort of trailed off.

Stanley and I didn't say anything. It had been five months, but neither of us were ready to work out the best response to people who said things like that.

"And I'm sorry it took me so long to get both of you here, but everybody just needed to make sure this was the right place for you."

He was being kind, but there was only one right place for us, and that was with Mum and Dad.

Uncle Hamish looked at me in the rear-view mirror. There was a pain behind his eyes. "You stick with each other, alright? Don't let silly arguments run on too long. You only have one brother."

It hadn't really occurred to me until that moment that Uncle Hamish had lost his brother and that he might be sad as well. I wanted to tell him I was sorry too, that it was going to be okay. It was going to be okay because it was only a temporary situation – Mum and Dad would turn up and everything would be fine. That while everyone else had said the chance of finding them all these months later was very small, it was still a chance. But I didn't trust myself to speak. Suddenly, there was too much sadness, and it was filling up the car, so I wound down the window to let some of it out.

Despite his daft name, Mr Dog must have been quite clever, because he nuzzled his nose into my lap like he sensed that I was in need of a hug. Which I was – conversations about Mum and Dad always left me needing a hug.

Stanley said, in a bit of an angry tone, "How long is this *wee* drive going to take, Hamish?"

Uncle Hamish said, "It takes as long as it takes," which was a very unclear answer, but neither of us pushed him to be more exact.

As it turned out, the wee drive from Edinburgh took FOR EVER. It was not a wee drive at all (unless you count all the toilet stops) but a very, very long drive, and it was dark by the time we reached Uncle Hamish's house by the loch. My bum was so numb from sitting on the wooden bench thing for hours and as I climbed out of the car on very stiff legs, I said, "I can't feel my bum, Uncle Hamish. I'm beginning to doubt whether it is still attached to me."

He laughed his booming laugh again. "Well, let's hope it is, we wouldn't want you to be known as Bumless-Benji." He carried our bags to the front door and said, "Here it is, the place your da grew up. I hope that, one day, you'll be able to feel happy here, and that it could be a home to you too."

I think Uncle Hamish must have registered the look on our faces, because he quickly added, "In time, of course."

Uncle Hamish's house was more like a big cabin, set a few metres up the hill, overlooking the loch and all the little holiday huts that people could rent out. It was built completely of wood with a veranda round the outside. Hanging from a post by the front door was a white-painted sign which said LOCH LOCHY HOLIDAY LETS – WHERE ADVENTURE HAPPENS!

Adventure – that sounded promising, although I was too exhausted from the very-not-wee journey to explore just then. But, despite my bum-numbing tiredness, I still felt a ripple of excitement when I saw the crescent moon reflected on the black waters of the loch and remembered the stories Dad had told us about Loch Lochy; as a boy, he'd thought there might have been a monster waiting in the deep. I decided right then and there that there was something about the place that felt mysterious, magical even. I've always had a good sense about these things.

I didn't argue when Uncle Hamish sent us straight to bed after fixing us a snack, which I was relieved turned out to be a cheese sandwich and not minced sheep lungs, heart and liver served inside a dead animal's stomach. Perhaps the information I had gathered on Scotland wasn't all that accurate. From what I'd seen at the station, no one had been wearing a kilt or white-and-blue face paint either.

After Stanley had turned out the light in our bedroom I said, "I have a feeling that it might be alright here, Stanley. Don't you think?"

I heard him turn over. "Nothing's ever going to be alright again, Benji. I think you need to get used to that."

I felt a little jolt of pain in my chest but clenched my jaw until it was gone. I wouldn't let Stanley be right. Dad always used to say, if you imagine positive things happening, they just might. Because I was the one with the excellent vision, and Stanley was a natural pessimist, I knew that if Mum and Dad were to be found, even after so many months, all the positive imagining would come down to me. I vowed I would never let the sadness take over.

CHAPTER 3

A ROOM WITH A VIEW OF THE ROBOT TADPOLE

Our room was up in the eaves of the house and was way bigger than any of the rooms in our house back in London. It smelled of new paint, which made me think Uncle Hamish had spruced it up especially for us. At the bottom of each of our beds, over the duvet, he had put a patchwork quilt – made by our Great-Grandmother Elsie, apparently. Stanley had let out a little grunting noise when he'd found out we were sharing, but I was really happy about it. I liked having him close by when the lights went out and my brain whirred. That first night at Uncle Hamish's there was a lot going on in my head and I found it really difficult to drift off.

I went over to the window to look at the stars twinkling over the loch. Because Stanley was making lots of snuffling snore noises, I had thought he was fast asleep. When he suddenly sat up and said, "Benji?" I banged my head on the glass, I was so surprised.

"Stanley! You made me headbutt the window!"

"What? How?"

"Because you made me jump."

"What are you doing out of bed?"

"I'm looking at the stars. Want to see?"

"Not really."

"Go on, they look amazing. I've never seen so many. It's like Scotland stole them all."

"Fine, I'll have a quick look." Stanley made a big show of getting out of bed and padded over to the window. He didn't say anything, but I could tell he was impressed.

"Do you remember when we were littler, and Dad woke us up in the middle of the night so we could go star watching?"

Stanley nodded, his eyes fixed on the night sky like he was searching for something.

"We went out into the garden in our pyjamas, and he made us lie down on the grass while he pointed out star constellations, like the robot tadpole."

Stanley shook his head and smiled. "Again, not the robot tadpole. It's called the Plough, or the Big Dipper if you're American." Stanley pointed. "Look, it's there. Do you see it?"

"Oh, yeah," I said but I hadn't. I could never make out shapes among the mass of stars. "And do you remember when that disc-shaped thing shot across the night sky and Dad started jumping about in his dressing gown and slippers shouting, *'We're lucky tonight, boys, what a treat! That was definitely an alien spaceship straight from the Tri-galaxy,'* do you remember that?"

Stanley sighed and said quietly, "I remember."

"We were so lucky, Stanley."

"We weren't lucky. Dad was winding you up, Benji. It wasn't an alien spaceship from the Tri-galaxy. It was more likely to be a plane or a satellite or a drone."

I feel a bit sorry for Stanley having no imagination. We'd obviously seen a spaceship, but that wasn't what

I'd meant. I'd meant we were so lucky to have a dad like ours.

When I opened my eyes the next morning, Mr Dog had his nose pressed up against mine. I don't know what Mr Dog had done in the night – maybe lick a badger's bottom? – but he had seriously terrible morning breath. Way worse than Stanley's even. I gave him a little pat. It was nice to have someone so close to me when the morning sadness hit. The moment when I remembered all over again. The storm. And the search. Stanley being found. And then the boat. But not Mum or Dad. That I wasn't home. That home didn't exist any more.

"You seem to have made a friend there," Uncle Hamish said. He was standing hunched over in the bedroom doorway, holding two cups. "Here, I brought you some milk. And breakfast is on the table when you're ready."

Stanley said, "We're not little kids, we don't drink milk," then he put his pillow over his face.

I think he was in one of his moods because he was

so tired. After we'd finished stargazing, we must have both fallen asleep, but he woke me up in the early hours. He'd had the sleep terrors again. He'd been having them ever since the accident. I'd tried to talk to him about it a bunch of times, but he wouldn't discuss it. There were a lot of things Stanley wouldn't talk about back then. But you don't need to be as clever as Stanley to work out what they were about, because he'd wake up gasping for breath and flapping his arms like he was trying not to drown.

"I'll have some milk," I said, because Uncle Hamish looked a bit disappointed and I was a bit thirsty, and it was nice to have a grown-up looking after us even if Stanley didn't realize it.

"Milk will help you grow up big and strong. Then maybe one day, like me, you'll be taller than your big brother." He did a little sad smile when he said that. "Although your da always managed to seem like the tallest man in any room he went into. I reckon it's character, not the length of your legs, that lifts you up."

Before I could wipe the milk off my top lip, Mr Dog did it for me with his big slobbery tongue, which was gross and nice at the same time. "Do you drink a lot of milk, Uncle Hamish?"

"Oh, aye. Used to drink three pints a day when I was a lad."

I thought about that for a moment. Character is all well and good for lifting you up, but I would like to *actually* be taller than Stanley one day, then I'd be able to pin him down and flob on his face like he used to do with me when we play-wrestled. But I wouldn't like to be FREAKY TALL like Uncle Hamish. No one wants to look like they spend the night bottling up children's dreams and eating snozzcumbers. I decided I'd limit myself to one pint, just to be safe.

"I'll leave you boys to get dressed. Breakfast is on the table downstairs and, once your bellies are nice and full, what do you say we take a look around the loch?"

"What's the Wi-Fi code? My phone hasn't got any signal," Stanley said, like he hadn't heard a word Uncle Hamish had just said.

Uncle Hamish frowned. "I'm not sure."

"You're not sure?" Stanley said that very rudely and if I'd been Uncle Hamish, I would definitely have had a word with Stanley about his attitude.

He didn't though, he smiled and said, "There's a gizmo box with it on in the study, but the signal isn't that great out here. I have a computer I use to take the online interweb bookings, the one I Zoomed you boys on. You can use that if you want."

I didn't want Stanley to spend hours online like he had been doing in London. "Can't you do that later, Stanley? Don't you want to go explore with me? It will be an adventure – I can feel it."

"Doubt it. And what's to explore? I already looked on Google Earth. There's a great big lake and a load of green hills."

"Oh, go on, please?" I was willing to beg. "An adventure is no fun on your own." I turned to Uncle Hamish, "No offence."

Uncle Hamish held up his hands. "None taken. Of course you want to explore with your brother. I understand that. Me and your da would spend hours outside on adventures."

I tried again. "What do you say, Stanley?"

Mr Dog padded over to Stanley's bed and put his

paw up on his knee. "See, Mr Dog wants you to, don't you, Mr Dog?" Mr Dog tilted his head and did a little whine to let Stanley know he really did.

"Oh, fine, whatever. Let's go and look at some water and some grass, it sounds spectacular."

Before I could tell him that he was being a bit of a Negative Norman, Uncle Hamish said, "It is **spectacular**. It's the most spectacular thing you will ever cast your eyeballs upon, laddie. You know, Loch Lochy is a magical and mysterious place. It gets into your soul."

I wasn't sure how a loch could get into your soul, but I was certainly up for it getting into mine and I definitely liked the sound of being somewhere magical and mysterious.

Uncle Hamish's eyes went a bit misty, and his voice broke as he said, "This place is the beating heart of the McLaughlin family. Always has been. Always will be. It's part of you both. You'll see that soon enough."

"I shall look forward to that," I said truthfully.

"Cut my veins, laddie, and loch water will spill out. This place will always belong to us McLaughlins. You mark my words." He sounded very determined when he said that. I could almost imagine him standing on top of a hill, kilt flapping, ready to fight off a rival clan.

Stanley got out of bed and marched out of the door saying, "If you want spectacular, you should spend some time on YouTube."

Uncle Hamish looked at me like I would be able to explain Stanley.

"He wasn't always like this. He used to be more fun."

Uncle Hamish put his hands on his hips and shook his head. "It must be very hard for your brother, what with him being there when it happened."

"He says he doesn't remember anything."

"Still..."

I don't think he knew quite what to say after that and I didn't want to speak any more about it, so we just stopped talking. It got a bit awkward, looking at each other and saying nothing, so I pulled my hoodie over my PJ top because it was a bit cold and said, "I think I might go and have some breakfast, if you don't mind."

"That", Uncle Hamish said, putting his giant hand on my shoulder, "sounds like an excellent idea, laddie."

CHAPTER 4

A KITCHEN THAT'S ALWAYS WARM

It turned out that breakfast wasn't that much of an excellent idea, as Uncle Hamish's idea of what constituted it was a bowl of something pale and sloppy-looking.

I made my way down the wooden staircase from our attic room and padded across the hallway rug, taking in the photos of the McLaughlin family. Some were black and white and looked really old; relatives I'd never met but I could see the family resemblance. I stopped still when I came to one of a young-looking Uncle Hamish with Mum and Dad. He was in the middle of them, his long arms slung over their shoulders. They were standing at the end of a jetty wearing swimming suits and the widest smiles. Even though I felt my stomach twist in pain, I couldn't help but smile back at them.

Uncle Hamish popped his head out of the kitchen doorway. "Ahh, there you are," he said, but he stopped when he saw what I was looking at.

"She used to love it here once upon a time." He sighed softly. "After she met Stuart, they'd spend every holiday in one of the cabins. She said the sky over Loch Lochy felt bigger, that she could really breathe here. She was a remarkable woman, your ma."

"Is," I said glaring at him, daring him to say otherwise.

He didn't say anything. He just held out his arms and said, "Come and get something in your belly, laddie."

I made my way into the kitchen. It was a big, warm room with one of those Aga cookers that always stays on. There was a rocking chair next to it and I imagined it would be a very nice place to sit in the winter. The kitchen cupboards were all wooden too and looked a bit old-fashioned. There were all manner of things piled up on a dresser: a drill and a spanner and letters and rubber bands and a couple of dog chews and a lot of flowery crockery, which I guessed had been passed down – I couldn't imagine Uncle Hamish picking that design himself.

Stanley was already sitting at the large wooden table with his nose turned up in disgust. "What is this... GRUEL?" he said when Uncle Hamish put our bowls in front of us.

"It's porridge," Uncle Hamish said.

Stanley held up his spoon and a big dollop of smush dropped into this bowl. "It tastes salty."

"That's because it's got salt in it." Uncle Hamish said it like putting salt on cereal was a perfectly reasonable thing to do.

I decided I should try it before I said anything because, who knows, salty porridge might be delicious. One mouthful quickly told me it wasn't. "Uncle Hamish, are you sure you read the recipe, because every taste bud on my tongue is telling me that salt should most definitely not be an ingredient in porridge," I said, trying to swallow my savoury oat slop.

Stanley pulled a very scowly face and said quite angrily, "This is truly awful." Then his scowly face sort of crumpled in on itself, and he said a little less angrily but a bit more sadly, "Everything is always going to be truly awful."

His words hung in the air for a while. I hated that Stanley had given up, that he believed what everybody else had told us – that five months at sea was too long.

Understandably, Uncle Hamish got really flustered after the truly awful for ever comment and started listing all the other things we could have while he frantically tried to clear the table, knocking things over in the process. "Me and your da used to eat it all the time when we were kids. I thought you might like it. I didn't mean...I am sorry...I just—"

"What we'd like is some regular cereal, like Cookie Crumbles," Stanley interrupted.

Salty porridge shot out of my nose when he said that. I was astounded! Mum had never let us have Cookie Crumbles cereal, because of the sugar content. She said that the cereal company could dress it up as much as they liked, but tiny biscuits were not a nutritious breakfast for two growing boys.

Stanley pushed his bowl away and picked up some letters from the table. He shoved them into Uncle Hamish's hands. "These came for you. They look important."

I don't know why he was embarrassed, but Uncle Hamish blushed as he took them and stuffed them into his back pocket. "Thanks – just junk mail."

"Really?" Stanley said. "I'd say you might want to see to those, they look urgent."

At the time, I wasn't sure why Stanley thought junk mail was urgent. Or why there was suddenly a strange atmosphere in the room, but I didn't mind because Uncle Hamish let us have two giant Wagon Wheel biscuits and a can of Fanta each to make up for the inedible porridge. I made a mental note that if ever he tried to give us haggis, I would be all dramatic like Stanley, claim everything would be awful for ever more, and try for a bar of Toblerone instead.

Upstairs, when we were changing into our clothes, I said, "Stanley, you're being a bit hard on Uncle Hamish, don't you think? He's let us come and live with him after all."

"Why do you call him that, *Uncle Hamish*?"

That seemed like a bit of a daft question, but I answered it anyway. "Because he's our uncle." Then I added a "duh" because I couldn't help myself.

"We barely know him. He and Dad had a massive falling-out and didn't speak for years, Benji! The only contact they had was via Christmas cards. And all we ever got from him were Scottish pound notes on our birthdays, which I'm not even sure is real money. I don't think that makes him our uncle. Just some Scottish bloke Dad didn't like and who probably doesn't want us here."

"Why did he say he'd have us then? Why did he go to all the effort with social services?"

"I don't know. Maybe he thinks he'll get money from

their will or something. I reckon dear old Uncle Hamish has some money troubles. That *junk mail* looked like final demands to me."

"Final demands?"

"He owes money, Benji. To all sorts of people. Banks, credit card companies, something called location services. He's up to his eyeballs in debt and it looks like he hasn't got long to pay it back."

It was possible, I supposed, that Uncle Hamish might have cash flow problems. But I believe it's right to think the best of people rather than the worst. "Look, he was Dad's brother and I think that means something. And, even though they fell out, did you ever hear Dad say a single bad word about him?"

I had him there and he knew it, so he didn't answer.

"Besides, we need someone to look after us and he is officially our guardian now, so you're just going to have to get used to it and stop being so mean and grumpy."

"I'm not grumpy!" he said, very grumpily. "I can look after you just fine. We don't need anybody else – not even Uncle Hamish."

For someone so intelligent, Stanley was saying a lot of supremely unintelligent things. Even I, with my visionary and strategic thinking, could see that an eleven-year-old kid and a thirteen-year-old kid probably needed a teeny bit of adult assistance, for things like transport and a place to live and getting things down from high shelves. Uncle Hamish would definitely be handy for that last one.

And, besides, I had a very positive feeling that Loch Lochy was going to be a good home for us, at least until Mum and Dad were found. I actually really liked Uncle Hamish, not to mention Mr Dog! And there was no denying there was *magic* and *mystery* in the air.

But Stanley probably couldn't feel that, on account of him being Stanley. I felt sure he would eventually, though.

People couldn't be sad for ever. Could they?

CHAPTER 5

A LOCH THAT WILL FIND ITS WAY INTO YOUR SOUL

The first time I clapped eyes on Loch Lochy in the daylight, in an instant, I understood what Uncle Hamish was saying about it getting into your soul. The still water was a dark, dark blue, a bit like the colour of Mum's eyes. The clouds which streaked the sky and the huge hills which stood around the edges were reflected on the surface of the water. As I looked out into the distance it was hard to see where the loch ended and the sky began. It was as though I'd walked straight into a painting by some really good painter. Not that Picasso though. We tried to paint like him at school and it was all colourful triangles, weird eye-lashed eyes and wonky noses.

"Bet you didn't get a view like this on your Google Earth," Uncle Hamish said.

Stanley just shrugged, probably because he couldn't argue with that.

"Sometimes," Uncle Hamish continued, "I struggle with the enormity of it all. That this all exists so perfectly, and that it can move me time and time again."

I didn't know quite what he meant, probably because he was being poetic, and as far as I can tell from all the poems I've ever read, poetry doesn't really make any sense. But if he was saying that he thought Loch Lochy was pretty awesome, I totally agreed.

"It's so quiet," I said.

"Too quiet, isn't that right, Hamish? Still no customers?" We turned round to see a man in a grey suit standing right behind us. He must have crept up very quietly for us not to have noticed him. His face was all pinched, like he was smelling a very disagreeable smell, and his dark glinty eyes were darting about all over the place, which made him look a bit like an angry pigeon. I did not like the look of him one bit.

"Gregor McGavin, as I live and breathe," Uncle Hamish said, unable to hide the disdain in his voice. "I thought I told you, you're not welcome on my property."

Gregor sniggered and raised an eyebrow. "Your property? You quite sure about that?"

Uncle Hamish just stared at him, not answering, so I said, "Course he's sure about that! He's lived here for ever. This place is in his soul!"

Gregor McGavin looked at me in the exact same way Stanley had looked at his salty porridge. Then he said, "He's got a mouth on him."

"Yes, I do," I said proudly, because speaking up is a very important thing to be able to do. We learned that in our PSHE lessons. "I have an excellent mouth."

Gregor McGavin looked confused for a moment, then turned back to Uncle Hamish. "You know the situation, Hamish. Time to accept it."

"*The situation*?" I mouthed at Stanley. What did that mean? Stanley shrugged again, but I could tell by the way that he was looking at Gregor McGavin all intently, that he was trying to suss him and **the situation** out.

Uncle Hamish took a step forward. His face had gone a purplish colour and his fists had curled up into tight balls. I thought, for a second, he might be about to punch Gregor, but he didn't, he said, "This place has belonged to the McLaughlins for generations. You'll never take it from me."

Uncle Hamish sounded very convincing when he said that, but Gregor McGavin did not seem to be that convinced.

He studied his fingernails like he really wasn't bothered about what Uncle Hamish had to say. "I can take it from you, and I will. You owe me a lot of money, Hamish."

Stanley was right! Uncle Hamish was in trouble. He shot me a *told you so* look, and I shot him my *this is not the time for gloating* look. Or at least that's what I was going for. It's quite a lot to convey with just your face, but I did my best.

Uncle Hamish jabbed his finger at Gregor. "I know it was you, spreading rumours that this place isn't fit for purpose. Scaring off people from staying here. That's slander and I'll have you for it!"

"You won't," Gregor sighed. "But it doesn't matter what *I* say. People can see for themselves this place is a dump. No one wants to come here, Hamish. Not when they've got a five-star luxury resort on the other side of the loch." He gestured wildly. "It must be a terrible burden all this. Let me take it off your hands. I'll flatten those sorry excuses for cabins and clear out the trees along the loch. I can do what you can't – make this place profitable. See sense, man, you're driving the place into the ground."

Uncle Hamish rose up to his full height – all six foot seven of him, and Mr Dog did a very supportive growl. "I've said you're not welcome on my property. Now are you going to leave, or do I have to make you?"

Gregor suddenly seemed to realize that there was an angry giant bearing down on him and he held up his hands and took a step back. This was a wise decision, because Uncle Hamish looked like he might actually swing for him. He was quite a terrifying sight, if I'm honest. Mr Dog, however, not so much. He was doing his best growling, but he couldn't help it that he had a very cute face.

"No need to get yourself worked up," Gregor McGavin said in a shaky voice, as he took a few more hurried steps backwards.

"Get off my land, you wee neep!"

Gregor McGavin took another few steps backwards.

"That's it, scarper!" Uncle Hamish boomed.

Realizing that it was probably the best thing to do, Gregor McGavin tried to scarper, but Uncle Hamish must have truly put the fear into him, because Gregor fell backwards and started flailing about on the floor like he was wrestling his own clothes. Eventually, he got to his feet, then he ran off back to his expensive-looking car. As he climbed in, he shouted, "You haven't heard the last of me, Hamish McLaughlin. This place will be mine, all mine!" Then he slammed his car door and drove off.

I don't know what came over me, maybe I just got caught up in all the drama, but I went, "WAH-HA-HA!" like some pantomime villain.

Uncle Hamish and Stanley looked at me like I'd lost my mind, which I suppose was a fair reaction.

Then Stanley said, very casually, "Well, he seemed nice. Friend of yours?"

Uncle Hamish's face became a little less purple. "I wouldn't exactly say that, no."

Stanley then looked Uncle Hamish right in the eye,

like he was daring him to lie. "Money a bit tight then? He said you owe him..."

Uncle Hamish hesitated, broke eye contact with Stanley, then gave us both a big smile that didn't quite reach his eyes. "Things are fine. Nothing for you two to worry about. Pay no attention to Gregor McGavin, he's a right wee walloper. A lying, cheating walloper!"

"Walloper?" Stanley said.

"You know, an eejit."

"I thought you said he was a wee neep?" I said.

"That too."

"What is a wee neep, Uncle Hamish?"

"A turnip – look, as I said, ignore him."

But I couldn't ignore Gregor McGavin, even if he was a right wee walloping turnip. I could tell Uncle Hamish was worried. People don't get as cross as he did if they're not worried.

"Are you going to lose the house and the holiday lets?" I looked at the deep never-ending blueness of the lake and then at all the little wooden huts set back from the shore, with their sweet little verandas and chequered curtains in the windows. Sure, they were a little run-down – actually, let's say well-used – but I reckoned they'd be about the best place ever to spend a holiday. I thought about all the families who would have stayed in them, making memories. And I imagined my dad running about the place when he was my age. He loved growing up here – he'd always said that. I looked down at my feet and wiggled my toes in my trainers. He could have stood on the very spot I was standing on now. He probably had. My heart skipped and I felt an overwhelming urge to lie down on the floor – to just be closer. But I didn't. Because that would have looked weird, even for me.

Instead, I said again, with more of a wobble in my voice, "You're not going to lose this place – are you? What would happen to me and Stanley if you did?"

"Nothing is going to happen to you because we're not going anywhere! This place has belonged to the McLaughlins for centuries and it always will. Now, enough of Gregor and his business, you should have some fun on your first day here. What do you fancy doing? You can go for a swim? It's July, the water will be warm. Ish."

It was a pretty obvious attempt to change the subject but Mr Dog, at least, didn't seem to realize. He must have recognized the word swim because he immediately raced towards the loch and launched himself into the water. It was a pretty good dive for a dog. Actually, it would have been a pretty good dive for a human. He bobbed to the surface and began paddling about with a very big grin on his little doggy face.

"Today's a swimming day, hey, Mr Dog?" Uncle Hamish said.

"Look at him go!" I said, thoughts of Gregor McGavin dissolving from my mind. "He looks like a dog-otter."

Uncle Hamish picked up a stick and chucked it

for Mr Dog to fetch. "He's a funny thing. Doesn't always like to go in. Sometimes he just stands on the bank, barking at the loch."

I peered down into the deep and felt an electric CRACKLE of excitement pulse through my body. "Maybe there *is* something in the water, like the Loch Ness Monster perhaps?"

"The Loch Ness Monster doesn't exist. It's an old Scottish legend," Stanley said, "and if it did, how do you think it would get from Loch Ness all the way over to here?"

"I don't know, fly maybe?"

Stanley said, "The Loch Ness Monster doesn't fly – it swims."

I grinned. "You admit it does exist then?"

"No! I'm not saying that. There's no such thing as the Loch Ness Monster."

"But you just said it swims."

Uncle Hamish laughed. "I wish we did have a flying Loch Lochy Monster, that would help get the tourists in. But no, there's nothing down there but rainbow trout, powan and bass. And the occasional eel. Mind you, your da always said there was something mysterious lurking in the loch."

"Those were just stories he told us when we were little. They weren't real," Stanley said.

I said, "You don't know that. Dad's always been very good at sensing those sorts of things."

"Has he now?" Uncle Hamish said.

"Oh yeah, he's very visionary. I take after him because I'm very visionary too."

Uncle Hamish ruffled my hair and laughed. "Is that right?"

"Maybe you could use all your vision to help Uncle Hamish with his money problems," Stanley said, very sarcastically.

Uncle Hamish's smile faded, and he said firmly, "I told you, I don't have any money problems." But he didn't look Stanley in the eye.

He wasn't very convincing. Even Mr Dog looked at him with a face that said he didn't believe a word of it. Uncle Hamish could pretend it wasn't happening all he wanted, but I knew he was in trouble and Stanley was right, I had the visionary skills to do something about it. We needed to be at Loch Lochy for when Mum and Dad came back. As Uncle Hamish was our only remaining relative, I was certain it would be the first place they'd come looking for us. Sure, he and Dad had fallen out, but brothers are always there for each other when it matters. Dad would know Uncle Hamish had come for us.

And besides, I'd had enough of things being taken from me. I might only have been here for a day, but I knew Loch Lochy was part of me, because it had been part of my dad. Loch Lochy belonged to the McLaughlins. The place was in our souls. No way was some pigeon-faced guy going to take it from us. No way. I decided there and then that I'd just have to come up with a plan. A way to make some money for Uncle Hamish. I could try and get the tourists back in, or maybe find some way to get Gregor McGavin to back off. I wasn't sure what exactly. But I'd think of something.

Although, if you had told me at the time what that plan would turn out to be, even if I'd been at my most visionary, I would have struggled to believe you.

CHAPTER 6

DONALDINA, IONA, ANNABEL, NESSA, PAISLEY, JOAN AND JACQUELINE, BONNIE AND FIONA

My plan for saving Loch Lochy from the grubby hands of Gregor McGavin did not get under way immediately, because I ended up having a massive row with Stanley.

We'd spent a bit of time skimming stones across the water. Well, Uncle Hamish and Stanley were skimming stones, I was more launching stones that dropped into the loch with a plop. Stanley managed seven skims which I thought had to be some kind of record, so I did a little victory dance on his behalf. But then Uncle Hamish got thirteen skims! Unbelievable! No dance could do that justice! He was quite apologetic, though, and tried to say to Stanley that he had had many years of practice.

While they skimmed and I plopped, I took the opportunity to ask about the holiday lets. Apparently, there were eight cabins, all named after long-since-departed female McLaughlin family members. There was a **Donaldina** – the biggest cabin; an **Iona**, where Mum and Dad used to stay; an **Annabel** – the smallest; a Nessa – which apparently a family of squirrels had claimed as home; a **Paisley** that had just about withstood a woodworm attack; a **Joan** and a **Jacqueline** that shared the same patio and were named after my great-great-aunts; and a **Bonnie** and a **Fiona**, that Uncle Hamish said were in better nick than the others. Usually, they'd be full at this time of year, but Uncle Hamish admitted to not having taken one booking. He blamed Gregor for scaring people off, but also admitted that the lets needed work, which required money. He was in the process of doing repair work himself, but he was just one man, and it was a big job.

"We'll help, won't we, Stanley?" I said.

Stanley shrugged. "Can't skim stones all day."

"True, but you two shouldn't be working. You should be settling in – relaxing. Finding your place here, you know?"

Uncle Hamish then suggested that we take a boat out on the water and, to me, that sounded like an excellent idea, but it turned out to be the cause of the row I had with Stanley. I imagined I'd be very good at loch boating, what with coming from a sailing family. I looked out over the loch and couldn't imagine anything better than being out on the water under the extra big sky. "Do you reckon we could row all the way to the other end?" It looked far, but not impossible.

Uncle Hamish laughed. Uncle Hamish, I realized, laughed a lot. Mainly at me, but I didn't mind because it made his eyes go all smiley-crinkly, just like Dad's.

"It's a bit far – almost nine miles – but I like your ambition, Benji."

"I do have excellent ambition." It wasn't the first time somebody had said that to me. "Dad used to say that you have to believe you can do something if you stand a chance of doing it. And although that wasn't the case with my French horn lessons, I definitely believe we could row to the other side. Don't you think, Stanley?"

Stanley obviously didn't think so because he glowered at me and said, "A boat, Benji, *really*?" He rammed his hands into his shorts' pockets and started back in the direction of the house.

"Stanley," Uncle Hamish called after him. "Stanley, come back, we can do something else. Anything you want! I'm sorry, lad, I should have realized!"

"I didn't think either," I said annoyed at myself. I ran after Stanley calling his name, but he didn't slow down. I only caught up with him when we were back inside.

"Stan, I'm sorry. Come back outside," I panted. Then, because I wasn't thinking properly, I blathered, "I just thought a loch, you know it's so calm, nothing like the sea and you love being out on the water, well you used to, and maybe this would be nice. Maybe good for you—"

"Nice?" He turned round and glared at me. "You have got to be kidding."

"Stanley, I'm sorry. Are you okay?" I said reaching out to touch his arm.

Stanley stepped out of the way and looked at me like I'd asked the stupidest question in the world. "Am I okay? Oh, I'm absolutely perfect, thanks for asking, Benji. Tip-top, except for you asking me to go out in a boat. Have you forgotten what happened the last time I went out in a boat?"

Of course I hadn't, but that was so different. That was a yacht and there'd been a terrible storm – it was a freak accident. And this was a loch. Dad's loch.

But I knew that he didn't want to talk about all that. I said, very quietly, so he knew I was sorry, "I haven't forgotten, Stanley."

He glared at me harder. "Well, it sounded like you did. It sounded like you'd completely forgotten the little matter of us not having any parents, because when you asked me if I was okay, it sort of seemed like you had."

"That's a horrible thing to say. Of course I haven't forgotten. I think about them all the time. I think about where they might be at this exact moment. About whether they're okay. If they're trying to get back to us. If they're stranded on some island somewhere. I still feel them and—"

He banged his fist against the wall before I could finish. "Don't start with that again. Why do you always have to go on about still feeling them?"

"But I do still feel them—"

"No, Benji. You don't. It's bad enough that we're being forced to live in the middle of nowhere with a less-hairy Hagrid, I really can't listen to you talking about how they might still be somewhere out there. You know what the police and the coastguard said? It's been too long. There's no hope. Why can't you get that into that head of yours?"

Stanley stormed off upstairs before I could tell him that even when there's nothing else and everything seems bleak and awful, there's always hope. Hope keeps things alive – isn't that what people say? So I had to keep hoping, because if I stopped hoping, it would mean that they really were gone, and I was not going to let that happen. Not then. Not ever.

CHAPTER 7

HIS TREE

After I heard the bedroom door slam, I leaned back against the wall and felt fully miserable. I hated arguing with Stanley. Uncle Hamish was right: brothers should stick together. But clearly, Stanley wanted to be on his own.

I wanted the old Stanley back. The Stanley who would always show up for me, his hand on my shoulder, if a bigger kid was being mean at school. The Stanley who would build dens behind the sofa with me, the Stanley who would lend me his games console. Actually, I don't think he ever did that last one, but you get the picture.

I closed my eyes and thought about Mum's super hugs. Her super hugs were the best. She'd squeeze us so tight that she'd squish our worries out of us, so it was hard to think about anything but her. And trying to breathe.

"The less-hairy Hagrid, hey?"

I opened my eyes, Uncle Hamish was standing in the doorway. "He didn't mean it, Uncle Hagrid, I mean Hamish."

"It's okay. He needs time. Perfectly understandable. He's been through a lot. You've both been through a lot. You're grieving."

I nodded, but I wasn't grieving. People might have thought I was, but you can't grieve for people if they aren't really dead. I was waiting. Waiting for them to come home and for things to be alright again.

I didn't want to think about what Stanley had said about Mum and Dad. Even all those months later, I was still not ready to listen to that, so I went outside and sat on the front steps of the house. I tried to distract myself by coming up with an idea of how to make Uncle Hamish a load of money, but my visionary talents weren't working at full throttle. I was half-heartedly throwing sticks for Mr Dog when Uncle Hamish found us and suggested that I take him out for a walk – Mr Dog, not Uncle Hamish.

I thought this was a highly irresponsible suggestion at first. In London, I'd never been allowed to go roaming the streets on my own. The streets can be scary for a kid. But rather than point this out and make Uncle Hamish feel bad, I said, "I don't really know my way round."

Uncle Hamish put his toolbox down on the ground. "Don't worry, Mr Dog does, and besides, if you stay on the track by the loch and don't deviate, you'll be able to turn round at any point and find your way back. You can see the house and the other holiday lets from most points on the path. I'd come with you, but I've got to sort out Donaldina."

"Who?"

"Not who, what."

"Oh! One of the cabins!" I said remembering. "What a name to call a cabin!"

Uncle Hamish narrowed his eyes, pretending to tell

me off, "After your great-aunt Donaldina. Anyway, she's got a problem with her plumbing and I'm the man to fix it."

"And a very lovely name it is too. Very sturdy sounding." I gave a little grin. "I'm sorry she's got a problem with her waterworks."

"Aye, art imitating life that," he said grinning back.

Then he picked up his toolbox, shook his head and, for a moment, the smile fell off his face and he suddenly looked like the thing that needed fixing the most.

"Things just keep going wrong around here. So many repairs to do, it's never-ending, Benji. Tell me, why would people choose to stay here when they could stay in a swanky apartment just over the way there at McGavin's?"

"Because people have to come here!" I threw my arms wide, "LOCH LOCHY HOLIDAY LETS – WHERE ADVENTURE HAPPENS! Isn't that what the sign says? You just need to spruce the place up a bit. Lick of paint, sort out Great-Aunt Donaldina's pipes and those squirrels squatting in Nessa, that's all. Ooh! And advertising! Yeah, that's what we need to do. Spread the word. A huge marketing campaign like the ones they do for Disneyland – except without all the fun rides and Disney characters – so not *exactly* like that, but you know what I mean! I'll think about it. Trust me, Uncle Hamish, I'll come up with something."

Uncle Hamish's smile found its way back to him. "You're a right wee barra, so you are, Benji McLaughlin! Now be off with you, laddie! This place won't explore itself!"

I still wasn't sure about heading off on my own and wished Stanley would come with me, but I didn't want to seem like a wimp. Mr Dog nudged my leg with his nose, like he was keen to get going.

Uncle Hamish had started off in the direction of Donaldina, so I chased after him. "Does he have a lead?"

"Mr Dog is not a lead kind of dog," he said, striding on.

"What if he runs off?"

Uncle Hamish stopped, which was good because he was hard to keep up with what with those enormo legs of his. "He won't run off. He likes you, I can tell."

I had thought the same thing about Mr Dog liking me. I don't want to sound like a **Benji-Big-Head**, but I know I am a likeable person because Mum told me I am, and it said so in my school report.

Anyway, Mr Dog seemed to be getting very impatient to go for a walk with me, because he started pushing my legs with his nose and whimpering. I didn't think I'd get anywhere trying to convince Stanley to come too so, very bravely, I decided that I would go it alone. Besides, as I looked down the path that twisted along the dark blue waters, the feeling of adventure rose up from my belly again, and everyone knows you must never ignore a feeling of adventure. Perhaps I'd be inspired even and come up with a brilliant money-making plan.

Uncle Hamish gave me the last Wagon Wheel from the packet, which I think he'd meant to eat because it was on top of his toolbox, but he said it would keep me going and promised he'd pop to the shops to get more for breakfast. I put it in my back pocket, as proper nourishment is very necessary when embarking on your first ever dog-walking adventure.

"Watch out for the jaggies," he shouted after us as Mr Dog and I set off.

I swung round. "The *what*?"

"Stinging nettles."

"Okay, we will!" Stingers, it turned out, were the least of my worries, but I didn't know that then.

As we made our way along the path, Mr Dog was the happiest I've ever seen a dog, ever. He kept jumping up and licking me to thank me, then he'd run off down the path to investigate a shadow or bark at a squirrel, then he'd run back and pounce on me again. Then he'd fling himself into the air – his ears spread out like aeroplane wings – and dive into the loch. He'd have a little paddle, his paws motoring like propellers, then he'd come out and stand right close to me and shake off all the water and I'd laugh, and he'd do it all again. I decided then that, despite his terrible morning breath, Mr Dog was by far the best dog I'd ever met.

Further down the track, there were some excellent climbing trees set back from the lake. Stanley and I had our very own excellent climbing tree in the park near us back in London, though we hadn't climbed it for ages. Stanley was probably either too old or too sad for climbing these days.

I took a moment to choose my tree and then I climbed up into the best-looking one. I shuffled along a big sturdy branch so I could eat my Wagon Wheel with a treetop loch view. I was about to take my first mallowy bite, but stopped when I spotted something carved into the trunk of the tree.

I don't know if my breath rushed into me or out of me.

"Oh, Stanley," I heard myself say. "You have to see this."

Two names, carved into the wood.

"Uncle Hamish," I whispered, touching the scarred bark and feeling how deep the letters had been cut. My fingers moved on, tracing

their way round the capital *S* of *Stuart* and ever so slowly looping round all the letters until I reached the final *t* and came to a stop.

Stuart. Dad. My dad.

Dad had sat in this tree. He'd been here – exactly where I was sitting. He'd sat on this very same branch with his brother, and they'd carved themselves into Loch Lochy for ever. I didn't know whether I was happy or sad or some other kind of emotion that no one has ever managed to come up with a name for, because it's too big to understand.

Marvin, the counsellor man back in London, had asked me to name my emotions in our sessions. I think I said what he wanted to hear in the end. But how can you even begin to know what to call some feelings? I could swallow a whole dictionary and I still don't think I'd find the words.

One thing I did know was that it was the closest I'd felt to Dad since he'd gone missing. The thought of Gregor McGavin cutting down Dad's tree made my insides burn. Uncle Hamish couldn't lose the place. He just couldn't.

I noticed something else carved below and pulled away some leaves to get a better look: WE WOZ 'ERE!

I let out the smallest of laughs. "Terrible spelling, Dad," I whispered.

I think I could have stayed there for hours, staring at his name and wishing on it, like it somehow had the magic to bring him back. But then Mr Dog ran up from the edge of the loch and started whimpering.

I looked down at his worried little face. "What's up, Mr Dog?"

Mr Dog whimpered some more, and I felt bad that dogs can't climb trees. He probably wanted to join me and enjoy the view. "You want to come up here too, don't you, Mr Dog?"

But he shook his head, turned back to face the loch and whimpered some more. This whimper was longer and louder. Like he was trying to tell me something.

Then he crouched back on his hind legs and started shaking. I realized he wasn't whimpering because he wanted to climb the tree, he was whimpering because he was scared. I looked out over the loch trying to work out what had given him the fear, but I couldn't see anything except still, calm waters.

"What's up, Mr Dog? What's the whining about?" I shuffled along the branch so I could shimmy down the trunk and give him a hug, because that's what you do when someone's scared of lochs, or weird shadows in their bedroom, or that they might not see their parents again.

I popped the last bit of Wagon Wheel in my mouth, touched my dad's name again, and then wrapped my arms round the tree to climb down. But just as I was finding my first foothold, I saw it.

A splash in the middle of the lake, right where the sun was shining. A huge splash. A monstrous splash. A splash so big, I had no doubt in my mind...it was a loch monster. It had to be! I felt something like an electric surge pulse from the waters right into my chest. I don't know, maybe it was my own excitement. Maybe it was

fear. Whatever it was, I was so surprised I forgot to hold on and fell straight to the ground. Luckily, my T-shirt snagged on a branch, so I didn't hit it with full force. I dangled for a bit, until my T-shirt ripped and then I dropped down.

I quickly jumped up, to see whether the monster was visible in the loch, but the waters were deadly still.

Mr Dog pushed his head between my legs. He'd stopped whimpering but he was still looking at the loch with suspicious doggy eyes. Clearly, Mr Dog had some kind of special doggy instinct that could detect loch monsters. It was all very mysterious and exciting, and I knew in that instant I had found the answer to all Uncle Hamish's money worries. He'd said it himself, a Loch Lochy Monster would definitely get the tourists in.

I raced back home as quickly as I could to tell Uncle Hamish and Stanley what Mr Dog and I had seen.

I burst in through the front door panting and sweating and shouted, "Loch in it! Mr Dog, saw. Scared! Ooooh. Ooooh. Very. Scared. Monster."

Uncle Hamish and Stanley were already sitting down for their lunch. They both looked at me like they didn't understand a word I was saying, which was understandable because I wasn't speaking in understandable sentences.

"*Ooooh. Ooooh?* What are you, a monkey?" Uncle Hamish asked.

I caught my breath and tried again. "Mr Dog and I saw a monster in the loch."

Stanley rolled his eyes. "Yeah right. What *exactly* did you see?"

I sat down next to him. "We did! Mr Dog suddenly got all scared and started whimpering and when I looked out at the water, I saw this massive splash. Only a monster could have made a splash that big!"

"So, what you're actually saying is that you saw a splash? You saw a splash of water in a loch? How unlikely." Stanley turned his attention back to his plate, clearly dismissing what I was saying.

"Not any old splash. A monster-sized splash!" I corrected.

"It certainly sounds like you had an exciting walk," Uncle Hamish said.

He was smiling but I could tell he didn't believe me either. "Don't you see, Uncle Hamish? A loch monster is the answer to your money-based prayers."

Uncle Hamish shifted in his seat. "I told you, there's no need for you to worry on that front."

He really wasn't understanding the significance of

what had just happened. And neither was Stanley, because he did a big long sigh and dropped his spoon into his noodle pot. "I knew he'd do this."

If he meant discover a way to save the Loch Lochy family home, he was right, but I could tell by his tone that was not what he was thinking, so I said, "Do what, Stanley?"

"Make up some nonsense about a monster living in the lake."

"It's not nonsense. I saw it with my very own eyeballs!"

"Could it have been a big fish?" Uncle Hamish asked, twirling his noodles around his fork, looking decidedly unconvinced. Frankly, I'd have thought he would have shown a tad more enthusiasm considering I had just found a way to save his home.

"Maybe it was a tuna fish," Stanley said. "Or salmon?"

"No way! Tuna aren't big! They fit in those little tins. And besides, it didn't feel like a fish. It felt all electricky, like a monster." To me, the evidence seemed pretty conclusive, but Stanley didn't seem to think so.

"You need to grow up, Benji, and stop believing in

things that don't exist and things that are never going to happen."

"*I* need to grow up? You're the one who was sulking like a six-year-old up in your room all morning."

"I wasn't sulking."

He *was* sulking.

"I was reading. And yes, you do need to grow up. You can't walk round with a head full of rubbish about water beasts or alien spaceships, or parents coming back from the dead."

"It's not rubbish!" I shouted, more loudly than I was expecting. "You're rubbish!" Okay, it wasn't the cleverest insult, but it was the best I could come up with when I was being so absolutely unbelieved in the face of some truly tremendous news.

"I'm not rubbish! You're rubbish!" Stanley shouted back at me.

I couldn't let that go, so I yelled, "Well, you're waaaaay rubbisher. You're the biggest rubbish there ever was. You great big rubbish head!" It really wasn't my moment for excellent put-downs, but I was quite worked up.

Uncle Hamish must have had enough of me and Stanley arguing because he suddenly jumped to his feet and his chair made a screech across the wooden floorboards. "Right, enough of all this rubbishness, hey, laddies? You two are brothers; you need each other."

Stanley mumbled, "That's rich coming from you."

If Uncle Hamish heard him, he didn't let on. Instead, he changed the subject and said, "Who's for some ice cream?"

Stanley dropped his cutlery onto the table. "I'm going back to my room. Suddenly I've lost my appetite."

As I watched him stomp upstairs, I wanted to shout out that he'd lost something way worse than his appetite – he'd lost his hope.

Stanley didn't believe in anything any more.

I decided then and there that I'd show him that things like alien spaceships and loch monsters and maybe even parents coming home safe were possible.

Well, maybe I wouldn't focus on the UFO thing.

It was at this exact moment that the first idea of a plan rippled through my mind, like a pebble dropping into a lake. What had Uncle Hamish said? That a Loch Lochy Monster would get the punters in? Well, we had a Loch Lochy Monster! I just needed proof and then to let people know about it. After that the guests would come flooding in just like they do at Loch Ness!

And if I could save the house and the holiday lets, and if I could prove to Stanley that there really was a Loch Lochy Monster, then maybe, just maybe, he'd start believing in things again. Maybe he'd have hope.

CHAPTER 8

MY BEDTIME PRAYERS

That night, once we had brushed our teeth and Stanley had finally finished his night-time poo, Uncle Hamish came upstairs to say goodnight. He stood stooped over in our bedroom doorway and watched while I knelt at my bed and said my bedtime prayers, first to God and then to Lord Vishnu and Lord Brahma. I've included them because we did Hinduism in Year 5 and discovered they are the gods of truth and protection. Who wouldn't want those fellas on their side?

Praying is a fairly new hobby of mine. Stanley thinks it's stupid because he doesn't believe in anybody's god, but that is because he needs evidence for everything. Which is fine, but a bit limiting. I took up praying after Mum and Dad disappeared, because I thought I may as well cover every possible avenue for help. With this in mind, I've also started to make sure I salute magpies and I never forget to wish when I blow an eyelash and, for Christmas, I know exactly what I'll be asking Santa for. I think it's called spread betting and I reckon it's an excellent approach because really, who knows where the power actually lies?

"How's your first day been?"

The way Uncle Hamish said that, with a little hesitation, made me think he genuinely wanted to know. That he wasn't just asking for the sake of asking. I took a moment to think about it because if a person really wants feedback, you should give it honestly. I had liked the Wagon Wheels for breakfast and walking on my own with Mr Dog. I had definitely enjoyed maybe, possibly, seeing a water monster. I also liked Uncle Hamish.

I tickled Mr Dog's ears; he'd curled up on the end of my bed like he meant to stay there. "I think today has been a great success, Uncle Hamish. I have had a brilliant time."

Uncle Hamish's smile stretched all the way to his big flappy ears. "I really hope that you boys will settle in okay here. I just want you to feel safe and looked after. And I know there was no will, but, like I said to that Sandra from social services, I truly, honestly believe with every fibre of my being, that this is where your parents would want you to be. I hope you come to love the place, just like they did."

"I hope so too," I said, although I probably already did love it, even with that scary monster in the loch. It would be a nice place to stay, a great place even, until Mum and Dad came back.

"How about you, Stanley? You're very quiet. How was your day?"

Stanley dampened the mood a bit by saying, "It was what it was."

I thought Uncle Hamish might be upset that Stanley hadn't been more positive in his feedback, but he took it well. He nodded, like he understood and said, "One day at a time, hey, laddie?"

Stanley just grunted. I hoped it was a friendly grunt, rather than a moody one, but there was no telling with him. His grunts all sound pretty much the same.

Uncle Hamish then decided this was the moment to drop an almighty bombshell about school. I stuck my finger in my ear and waggled it about madly, because I thought I must have been hearing things.

"What do you mean we only have four weeks of the school holidays left? That is outrageous!" It wasn't even the end of July, how could the summer holidays be ending in four weeks?

"That's when the Scottish summer holidays end," Uncle Hamish said, very matter-of-factly.

Forgetting about haggis and the no-underpants-kilt thing, I had liked what I'd learned about Scotland, right up until that point.

I'd had visions of spending the whole six weeks of the summer holiday hunting for loch monsters and saving Uncle Hamish's home for him. Dad's home too. I did not have a single vision where I'd be studying Maths and English. I didn't even know if they taught English in Scotland. Maybe I'd be learning SCOTTISH.

I didn't know any Scottish. I'd be right at the bottom of the class.

But worse than that, if I couldn't get the tourists in, because I was sat behind some desk trying to learn another language, Uncle Hamish would lose the place and that just wasn't happening. Not on my watch.

Uncle Hamish tried to put a positive spin on it. "I think school will be good for you, you'll get to meet some of the local kids, make some friends."

"That is true," I said, reminding myself not to think negatively. I'd just have to save Loch Lochy before term started. I could do that. Mum always told me that I can do anything I put my mind to and, although she probably was a little bit biased, I'm inclined to agree with her.

"I wish, just for once," Stanley said, "that people would stop telling us what would be good for us."

"But friends *would* be good for us," I said.

"We've got friends, back in London," Stanley said.

"But you stopped talking to them after it happened, Stan. I think we may as well give some new ones a try."

"I'm glad you think that, Benji, because I've asked

Clara, a friend of mine, to bring her daughter, Murdina, round."

I looked at Stanley and mouthed, *"Murdina?"* It didn't sound like a particularly peaceful name. A bit murdery in fact. Stanley raised his eyebrows, so I reckon he was thinking the same thing.

"It will be nice for you to know someone when you go to school. She'll be starting P7 with you. Poor wee lassie, I think she had a bit of a hard time with some kids last year and Clara thinks it would be good for her to make some new friends too."

Uncle Hamish had delivered a lot of information that needed unpacking.

"What is P7 and who is this Clara? Is she your girlfriend? And what kind of name is Murdina? And why doesn't she have any friends?"

"P7 is the same as Year 6 and no, Clara's not my girlfriend. She was married to my sort-of pal Duncan, but now she's a friend and my financial advisor – although I don't pay her to be either of those things. And Murdina is a Scottish name."

"Wow, Scottish people really have an interesting

approach to naming things."

Uncle Hamish laughed. "She's a lovely girl – a very colourful imagination, a bit like her da. I'm sure you'll get on."

Frankly, I was sceptical. There must be some reason she'd fallen out with the kids in her class, but I told myself not to be too judgy. Sometimes that's not as easy as it sounds.

Just as Uncle Hamish turned to leave, I said, "Does she know why we're here? What happened?"

Uncle Hamish spoke gently. "Aye, she does. Clara helped me with all the hundreds of forms I had to fill out to get you here. But don't worry, Murdy won't go blathering about it, okay?"

"Okay," I said. To be honest, I was quite glad she already knew. It meant I didn't have to struggle with trying to tell her.

Once the lights were turned out, I tried to tell Stanley about Dad's name being carved in the tree, but I think he was still a bit annoyed with me about the boat thing and about the fact I was insisting that I had most probably definitely seen a monster, and he didn't want to listen.

I tried my best to apologize but it all went a bit wrong. I said, "I'm sorry about asking you to go out on the water. Maybe it would help, you know, if you talk about what happened that day."

"I'm not scared of the water, alright? I just didn't want to go out on a boat. It's no big deal. I don't want to talk about it. And I've told you, I don't know what happened. I don't remember anything, and I wish you'd stop asking. Now, just go to sleep."

He sounded really cross, so I knew he was probably lying. He was scared. I wished I knew what was going on in his head and why he wouldn't talk about things. Stanley had never been that much of a talker, not like me, but he'd got even more quiet since Mum and Dad disappeared. He'd never spoken about what he saw. Not to me, not to his counsellor. Maybe he didn't have the right words either. Maybe he was more honest about that than me.

Mr Dog must have sensed that Stanley was in need of a pal, because he got down off my bed and went and put his face up on Stanley's pillow. Stanley just rolled himself up in his duvet and turned away.

I thought about going over and trying to give Stanley a hug myself, and even though I wanted to so badly, I just didn't think I could. I knew I couldn't face him turning away from me as bravely as Mr Dog had.

I said, "Here, boy, come," and Mr Dog gave Stanley a friendly sniff, then jumped back onto my bed. I buried my face in his slightly smelly fur and cuddled him tight instead.

CHAPTER 9

MEETING MURDY

The next morning, I woke up to find Stanley was already downstairs eating his breakfast. While I was disappointed for me to see that it was toast and not Wagon Wheels, I was pleased for Uncle Hamish that he had already improved his adulting so soon.

"Morning, sleepyhead, you'd better eat and get dressed. Clara and Murdina will be here soon."

I sat down at the table and grabbed myself an extra buttery slice.

"I know you were keen yesterday, Benji," Uncle Hamish continued, "so I thought maybe you and Murdy might want to take a boat out. Stanley – obviously no pressure for you to do anything. But, Benji, Murdy loves a paddle, so if you want to get out on the loch, this is your chance. Just make sure you put on a life jacket. I know you're a strong swimmer – but best to be safe, hey?"

I think Uncle Hamish mentioned the life jackets for Stanley's benefit, to reassure him, but as I wasn't sure I wanted to be out in the middle of a loch with a girl called Murdina, I'd definitely be wearing one. What if she lived up to her name and chucked me overboard or came at me with an oar or something?

"She is alright, isn't she, this Murdy?" I asked nervously.

"Yes, and there's no need to pull a face when you say her name, Benji," Uncle Hamish said. "She's very nice. I'm certain you'll both like her."

"Stanley, do you want to—" I started but he cut me off straight away.

"Why would I want to hang out with a couple of primary-school kids?" Stanley said, angrily munching on his toast.

That annoyed me. How could he say we only needed

each other one minute and that he didn't want to be around me the next? "Why do you always have to be so mean, Stanley? What did I ever do to you?"

Stanley looked a bit surprised for a moment, like he hadn't realized that what he had said would upset me. I guess he was too busy thinking about how he was feeling to worry about how his words might have hurt. Or maybe he'd just got used to being grumpy.

He swallowed his toast, then said a little more kindly, "I just don't fancy it. But don't let me stop you."

Uncle Hamish drained his milk – which I'm really not sure he still needs considering his epic size – clapped his spade-sized hands and rubbed them together. "They'll be here soon, why don't you two eat up and go and get changed."

I was just putting my socks on when Stanley and I heard voices downstairs.

"They're here," I said.

Stanley groaned. "I really, really can't be bothered with this."

I couldn't remember the last time he'd been bothered about anything and even though I was a bit worried about meeting Murdina, I told myself I would have to be positive for both of us. I pulled on my trainers and said, "You never know, she might be alright."

Uncle Hamish hollered up the stairs, "Benji, Stanley, come down here, would you? There are some people I'd like you to meet."

"Be down in a minute!" I called back.

Stanley shut his book and sat up. "Come on then, we may as well get this over with."

When we got downstairs there was no sign of Murdina, but a woman, who I guessed was Clara, had her hand on Uncle Hamish's shoulder and a look of concern on her face. She was wearing denim dungarees, which I had not expected from a financial advisor, and had shiny long dark hair, twinkly brown eyes and was Chinese. Whatever she and Uncle Hamish were talking about, they quickly stopped when they saw us, but I just caught her saying, "I know it's difficult, but you can't afford to keep paying that out, Hamish."

Uncle Hamish rearranged his face into a smile and said, "And here they are, my incredible nephews. Have you ever clapped eyes on a finer pair?"

"I haven't!" Clara held out her hand and we shook it in turn. "Murdy's very excited to meet you both. It will be good for her to make some new friends," she went on. "She's outside throwing sticks to that hound of yours. Why don't you go and say hello?"

I didn't like this twinkly-eyed Clara calling Mr Dog, the most excellent dog on the planet, a hound and I didn't like the fact that this Murdina girl was outside playing with him without me. I looked at Stanley and said quite forcefully. "Are you coming?"

He said, "Yeah," but his face said he'd rather be chewing his own toenails.

Murdina and Mr Dog were on the front path that ran alongside the holiday lets. As I stepped outside, I took a moment to take in Loch Lochy again. It was beautiful. True, the little wooden cabins looked a bit tired and sad, but all they needed was a little bit of love and attention. I felt confident that with the correct **Benji McLaughlin rescue plan**, people would come to stay again.

Mr Dog, the traitor, looked like he was having a wonderful time, his doggy tail was wagging as he leaped to catch sticks out of the air. I was a bit surprised to see that Murdina didn't look in the least bit **murdery**. She was wearing a deep purple top and shorts that were actually quite cheerful. She was small and skinny and had tied her scruffy dark hair on top of her head with a green scrunchie, which made her look a bit like a **beetroot**, and beetroots really don't look that deadly.

"Hi," I said, "you must be Murdina—"

"It's Murdy, actually."

"Okay, hi, Murdy. I'm Benji and this is my older brother Stanley."

Stanley did one of his hello grunts.

She pointed at me, then looked me up and down. "How old are you? Mum said you were starting P7 with me, but you look too small for P7."

That was outrageous! "I'm taller than you!"

"No, you're not."

Uncle Hamish was right about her colourful imagination. "I am," I shot back.

She grabbed hold of me, turned me round and pressed her back against mine.

"Oi, you," she said to Stanley, "who's taller?"

Even though I had not agreed to a measure off, I wasn't about to lose it to a human salad item, and I stretched my spine so I was as tall as I could possibly be.

Stanley completely betrayed me by saying, "Sorry, Benji, but she has it."

"You can't count the top of her hair, that's giving her at least another eight centimetres."

"He can count my hair, it's part of me, isn't it?"

Frankly, that was the most ridiculous thing I'd ever heard. "That's not how it works. Tell her, Stanley!"

Stanley then completely betrayed me for a second time by saying, "Dunno, might be a different way of measuring in Scotland," when he absolutely knew there wasn't a different way of measuring in Scotland.

Murdy folded her arms and said, "Now that's sorted, what are we going to do? My mum promised me that you two would be fun. I could have gone roller skating with Kay McGavin and the twins – Clarissa and Camilla Barclay – the most popular gang in school, but instead I had to come here."

"Hang on – Kay McGavin as in Gregor McGavin?" I asked.

"Yup, Kay's his daughter."

"And she's a friend of yours?"

Murdy shifted from foot to foot and said, "She's in my class." Which I took to mean no. Something about her voice made me think she'd never had an invite to go roller skating.

"Anyway," she said, "I'm here now so how are you going to entertain me?"

Stanley and I looked at each other. I suddenly felt under a LOT of pressure to suggest something excellent. She stood with her hands on her hips, tapping her foot with her spring-oniony topknot bobbling about. "Well? Or don't you English kids know how to have fun?"

Making it a matter of national pride only added to the pressure. "Umm, Uncle Hamish thought we could take a boat out? He said you liked that."

She stared at me for a moment, and I thought maybe I'd let both myself and England down, but then she pointed at me and shouted. "Boats are good but keep talking – what are we going to do in a boat?"

"Sit in it?"

"Obviously, but what else?"

"We can go loch-monster spotting?" I said, then immediately regretted it.

Stanley let out a big groan. "You've got to be kidding me. This again?"

Clearly, he wasn't impressed, but Murdy was staring at me with big open eyes. "What did you just say?"

I gulped. "I said we could go monster spotting."

"Monster spotting?" Her eyes narrowed. "What do you know about monsters?"

"Not much, but I'm keen to find out! Hang on, what do *you* know about monsters?"

I hadn't meant to sound like I was challenging her, but her face suddenly clouded over. "Are you teasing me? If you're teasing me, I'll run right through you."

I didn't like the idea of being run through, whatever that meant. My voice got stuck somewhere near my tonsils for a second and when I did get the words out, they were a little bit squeaky. "You see, I think I saw one."

"You think you saw one?" Murdy said, slowly.

Stanley did such a big sigh I was surprised his whole body didn't deflate. "He didn't see one. He's making it up."

Murdy held up her finger and shushed Stanley. "Carry on, Benji."

I cleared my throat and searched for a lower pitch. "Yes, I think I saw one."

She looked at me suspiciously. "What did people tell you about me? What did they say?"

"Er, nothing. Uncle Hamish said you were nice." He was clearly way off with that, but I didn't point it out.

"No one mentioned anything about me and the Loch Lochy Monster?"

"What about you and the Loch Lochy Monster?" I asked, suddenly very interested.

"That I've seen it too."

CHAPTER 10

ON THE WATER

Murdy started off towards the rowing boats which were moored by the edge of the lake, with Mr Dog right by her side, leaving me processing this enormous piece of information. I must have been standing with my mouth open because Stanley said to me, "Close your mouth, it makes you look a bit gormless."

"Did you hear what she just said, Stanley? She said she's seen the Loch Lochy Monster! Didn't I tell you it was real?"

He rolled his eyes. "You really are the most gullible person I have ever met. She's clearly winding you up. Or she's as delusional as you."

"I think she sounded like she was telling the truth."

"There's no such thing as monsters, Benji."

By the time we got to the boat, Murdy already had it halfway in the water and Mr Dog was sitting at the bow with his tongue hanging out, like a big slobbery figurehead.

"What do you mean, you've seen a loch monster?" I asked.

"I told you, she hasn't seen it," Stanley said a little too wearily for my liking.

"Think what you like. Anyway, how do you know what I have and haven't seen?" Murdy said that in a very casual way. She didn't seem to care whether Stanley believed her or not, which only made me believe her more. She handed me the oars. "Get in, I'll push the boat into the water."

"Why?" I asked.

"Because we're going Loch Lochy Monster hunting. If it's here, I want to see it. Besides, it will be fun! Now would you get in already?"

I was about to do as I was told but thought better of it. I didn't want there to be a power struggle and it had been *my* idea to go monster hunting. Very politely, I said, "No, it's okay. You can get in and *I'll* push the boat into the water."

Murdy didn't seem to feel the need to be polite because she said, "Away and boil your head. You're not going to be able to push the boat in with your **wee noodly arms**. Get in."

I looked at Stanley. "Did she just tell me to go and boil my head?"

He nodded. "I think she did."

Murdy said, "I'll boil it for you myself if you don't hurry up. Are you two coming, or not?"

Stanley stared across the water, and I saw his expression change. He was suddenly the one who looked small, and I felt the same overwhelming urge to hug him like I had the night before.

"I...I...don't think so," he said.

"You...you...don't think so?" Murdy mimicked.

Stanley recovered himself and smiled. "While it is difficult to refuse such a warm invitation, I'll watch you both from here. Much safer – no loch monsters on dry land."

He said that second part very sarcastically, but Murdy didn't seem bothered. "Suit yourself. Just me and **wee-man-noodly-arms**."

I knew that it wasn't the monster in the loch Stanley was worried about, it was the monsters in his head. But it didn't seem fair to bring it up in front of Murdy. Besides, I couldn't have her believing the English were afraid of the water. So, I didn't say anything to Stanley then and climbed into the boat. "I do not have **noodly** arms by the way, Murdy. They are actually very strong arms."

She shoved the boat into the loch then jumped on board. "They look like **noodly** arms to me. We can arm-wrestle later if you want to prove me wrong."

I said, "You name the time and place," so I didn't seem like a chicken, although I had zero intention of ever arm-wrestling her, just in case she did win.

She smiled, like she'd worked out I was bluffing. "Thought as much. Now, are you going to start rowing or are you just holding on to those oars for decoration?"

I hadn't rowed a boat before; our boat had been a sailing boat, and if we ever went out in the dinghy, Dad had always taken the oars. He had made it look so easy.

I had NOT reckoned on it being quite so impossibly tricky. The oars were *so* heavy, but I knew if I admitted that to Murdy, she'd think she was right about my noodly arms and she really wasn't.

Dad used to say that when you find something difficult, it's best to attack it head on. So that's what I did. I attacked the oaring with all the power I could summon. I thrashed about trying to get the boat to move and my arms to work in time. They were finding that very hard to do, but eventually, thanks to my

superb effort and unwavering self-belief, we finally began to move.

Unfortunately, it was round in circles, but it was a start.

"What are you doing?" Murdy spluttered.

"I'm oaring – what do you think I'm doing?"

Unhelpfully, Stanley shouted over, "You alright, Benji? You look a bit lost? Could you do with a map?"

"I'm just getting my muscles warmed up, actually. A good warm-up is very important before you do any exercise, or you might pull a muscle."

"You need to have muscles to pull them," Murdy said.

I stopped oaring at that point. There really is only so much one boy can take. "You, young lady, are very rude and have a very poor attitude and I think you should be a much better representative for Scotland, if I'm being honest."

She stared at me blankly for a moment. She was obviously taking on board what I was saying. I folded my arms, feeling very pleased about standing up to her, and waited for an apology.

An apology did not come.

Instead, Murdy burst out laughing and saying, "You, young lady," over and over again in the worst English accent I have ever heard.

I was beginning to doubt whether she was the best person to go loch-monster hunting with, but my choices were extremely limited and, although for different reasons, Uncle Hamish and Stanley were depending on me to find one.

Even if they didn't know it.

CHAPTER 11

SEARCHING A MONSTER

To be honest, there was a bit of a power struggle in the boat that first time Murdy set sail. In the end, after a bit of oar-grabbing, a lot of arguing and a near capsizing, Mr Dog finally lost patience and growled at us. I could tell he was disappointed by our lack of teamwork, so I said to Murdy, "Shall we take an oar each?" and Mr Dog nodded his head in approval.

It turned out that Murdy and I were much better at rowing the boat together than on our own. In fact, once we got into a rhythm, even she had to agree we were quite speedy. Mr Dog stood proudly at the front, his flappy ears streaming out behind him like furry flags.

Soon we were way out almost in the middle of the loch, heading to where I had spotted the monster, and, very quickly, Stanley had become a sad little dot on the horizon. Actually, he looked more like a sad little comma because he was hunched over, but you know what I mean.

"Let's stop here for a little rest," Murdy said, lying back and tilting her head up towards the sun. It was a bright day and the wood of the boat felt warm under my bum cheeks. A warm bum is always a nice feeling (unless it's a warm and wet bum – that is the exact opposite of a nice feeling).

I looked about, taking in my surroundings. There was no denying it was a beautiful place. I spotted Dad's tree and smiled. "This is about where I saw the Loch Monster," I said.

Murdy opened one eye and looked around. "Doesn't look like your monster's here today."

She was right, it really was very peaceful. But I didn't want peace, I wanted a monster and we were on a schedule. School would start before I knew it – we didn't have time to lounge about in the sun. Especially with Gregor McGavin breathing down Uncle Hamish's neck.

"Okay, Murdy, tell me everything you know about THE LOCH LOCHY MONSTER."

She closed her eyes when she spoke. "Er...I don't know very much, to be honest. Other than I saw something in the water a few times that didn't look like anything I'd ever seen before. It's hard to describe. And when I did try to describe it, nobody believed me. Said I was making it up, that it never happened."

"Some people have no vision."

She shrugged. "For sure."

"Was it big?"

"I should think so."

"What colour was it?"

"I don't know, I would imagine a monster would be dark in colour, wouldn't you?"

I would. I dipped my hand in the water and imagined a huge dark creature prowling the waters below. I did a little shiver of fearful excitement and pulled my hand out again. "When did you see it?"

She sighed. "I can't remember exactly, maybe a

couple of years ago."

"We need to find it again. It's important. Did you know Uncle Hamish might lose his home?"

Murdy propped herself up on her elbow and swatted away a midge. "Mum says he can't afford to keep the holiday lets on without any holiday-letters. Gregor McGavin has been after his place for years. It's why he and your uncle fell out. Mum thinks that Gregor was responsible for all the bad reviews and the awful report in the newspaper."

"What awful report?"

"Oh, just that the place was run-down, unhygienic and unsafe. Reviews like that can kill a business."

"Uncle Hamish said it was nothing to worry about, but I know he's in big trouble."

"If he lost this place, Mum says it would be like losing his world."

"Losing your world is a very terrible thing," I said. Stanley and I both knew that.

"It sure is," Murdy said sadly. At the time, I thought she was being sympathetic, and I think she was, but I know now she was talking about her world too.

"I'm not going to let it happen," I said.

She tilted her head and frowned. "How are you going to stop it? No one visits here any more. Mum says Hamish's business is dead in the water – he can't compete with those lush apartments the McGavins have over on their side. Gregor wants to expand over here and the McGavins always get what they want. She thinks it's time for your uncle to face facts."

To me it seemed like Murdy's mum said a lot of things that she knew nothing about. Didn't she know loch water ran in Uncle Hamish's veins?

"Everyone will want to come when they hear about the Loch Lochy Monster! I read about the monster at Loch Ness before we moved up here. Tourists come from far and wide wanting to catch a glimpse of the thing. Like whale watching, with much less certainty but much more hope and vision, which, in my opinion, makes it much better! I'll pack this place out with tourists, then Uncle Hamish will be able to pay off rotten old Gregor McGavin."

Murdy studied my face as though she was trying to work out if I was serious. "*That's* your plan? Believe me, you can't go about here talking of the Loch Lochy Monster. People will think you've gone crazy or that you're a liar or make out you're attention seeking because your dad left you."

"Well, that's my plan, and it's a good one. *And* for your information, my dad didn't leave me. He'd be with me if he could." I said that quite snottily because, at the time, I hadn't realized she was talking about *her* dad. I suppose for someone so visionary, I can be pretty blinkered sometimes.

Murdy didn't pull me up on it. Instead she looked at me with big, sympathetic eyes and said, "I'm sorry – you know – about your parents. It must be awful. How did it happen?"

It was awful but I didn't want to talk about it with her, so I just shrugged and said, "I'd rather not talk about it, it's just something that happened," which might have come across as a bit uncaring on the surface. But deep down I felt the hurt pulsing in me.

I didn't want to cry, not in front of her, and I was annoyed that she made me think about the sadness. So, I said quite crossly, "If you want to point me in the direction of the Loch Lochy Monster, that would be much appreciated."

Murdy smiled. "I can't just *point you in the direction* of the Loch Lochy Monster."

"Why not?"

"Because the loch monster doesn't have an address, you numpty. It just shows up."

It felt like she was being unnecessarily difficult, and my annoyance was growing. "Just show me where you last saw it. *If* you remember. *If* you actually saw it."

Her eyes narrowed in a quite an unnerving way. "Are you calling me a liar?" She turned away and muttered loud enough for me to hear her say, "You're as bad as the rest of them."

She was angry, but I could tell she was also upset. I *had* basically called her a liar, which wasn't very nice. In my defence, she had called me a numpty, so it was sort of deserved. But I know better than anyone what it feels like not to be believed. I needed to come up with an apology that let her know I was sorry, but also ensured she understood her part in the argument.

But it was hard to think straight because my mind

kept turning back to Mum and Dad and I hadn't got very far into working out how an apology like that would sound, when Mr Dog suddenly backed into my legs and started growling, low and loud.

The sudden change in him made my stomach flip.

I put my hand on his head and said, "Hey, Mr Dog, what's up, boy?" But I already knew.

Mr Dog growled some more, his eyes fixed on the water.

A shiver ran from the backs of my knees all the way up to my ear lobes. Something...something was happening.

"It's here," I whispered. I could feel it. I really could.

"What's here?" Murdy asked.

"The Loch Lochy Monster."

CHAPTER 12

RIPPLES ON THE LOCH

"The Loch Lochy Monster?" Murdy jumped to her feet, making the boat rock. "It's here?" she shouted, a look of mad confusion in her eyes. "Really? Where?"

I wasn't exactly sure of its precise location, but because of my very good sense for detecting magical and mysterious things, like loch monsters, I was certain it was near. Probably. "Yes, the Loch Lochy Monster is near, I can feel it. Can you feel it?"

Mr Dog whimpered, just like he had the day before, to let us both know he could feel it.

Murdy, who obviously didn't have monster-sensing-senses as superior as mine said, "Feel what exactly?

How can you feel a monster?" Then she whipped her head about, scanning the surface of the water. "I don't see anything. Are you sure? Do you see anything?"

"No, but I fe—"

"Enough of the feelings, birdbrain. Do you *see* anything?"

I didn't. The water was flat and calm, but I was beginning to think it had grown darker. Something was happening. I knew it and Mr Dog knew it too. His growl grew lower and his whole body seemed to be vibrating.

"Sorry, Mr Dog," Murdy said, giving him a stroke, "are we scaring you?"

"It's not *us*, Murdy! It's the monster he's scared of!"

For a moment, she looked like she was studying my face, trying to work something out, but then she tilted her head and I swear I saw a small smile twitching on her lips – almost like she was enjoying herself.

"Come on, monster!" she shouted, some might say bravely, I would say stupidly. "Show yourself. Benji has a plan in mind for you!"

"Yeah, monster, show yourself," I said, nowhere near as forcefully as Murdy.

I have to admit, at this point, I was beginning to have doubts about whether I actually wanted to see a loch monster so close up. It suddenly seemed a much better idea to see it from a little further away. Like from the window of my bedroom, for example.

But there was no time to think about that, because a large ripple spread out around the boat.

"Woah! Did you see that?" I asked.

Murdy frowned. "See what?"

"That ripple?"

Murdy's smile fell away, and slowly a smile formed on her lips. "Oh yeah, a *ripple*. I saw it. Of course, I did." Her eyes began to twinkle with excitement. "It was big. Really big!"

"So's that one," I said as another ripple emerged from underneath us.

Murdy looked at the water then at me. "Oh yeah, huge!"

It must have all got a bit too much for Mr Dog. He stopped growling and cowered under the seat, with his tail tucked between his legs. I considered joining him, but I couldn't tear my eyes off the water as another ripple rose up from under us, quickly followed by another, and another. I did an involuntary swallowy-gulp thing, because there was a lot of scary rippling going on and I was one hundred per cent certain I knew what was causing it.

"Do you think it's un…" My voice trailed off because something far more worrying than the rippling was happening. The water around us began to churn, like it was being boiled.

"Underneath us?" Murdy looked at me, her eyes practically popping out of their sockets, and whispered, "Yeah, maybe!"

I couldn't be sure, but she sounded more exhilarated than frightened. The boat began to rock more violently and a little whimpering noise escaped my lips. I grabbed the sides to stop myself falling in. Desperately, I glanced back to shore to see if Stanley was still there, in case he needed to summon a rescue team but, selfishly, he'd gone back indoors.

When I turned back round, I was surprised to discover Murdy had lowered herself onto her knees and was peering over the front of the boat, so her nose was practically touching the water. "I don't see anything. Do you see anything?"

"Get away from the edge, you're going to fall in! That or have your face ripped off by a terrifying loch monster."

"I'm not going to fall in! I'm just looking that's all!" She swung round, scrambled along the boat and kicked me in the head as she climbed over me, saying, "Get your wee self out the way, I want to look out the back." Why she wasn't concerned about having her face removed, I do not know.

I looked around anxiously. The waves around us were getting so big, they were starting to lap over the sides. Mr Dog, unable to hide under the seat due to the violent motion of the boat, was turning round in circles and barking really loudly.

"It has to be right underneath us." Murdy was leaning so far over the back of the boat with her purple bum stuck in the air, that I knew there was no way she wasn't going to fall in. "Hold my legs so I can put my face into the water."

Of all the ideas she could have come up with, I think

that putting her face in the water had to be the worst.

"Or maybe," I said, "we could grab the oars and row back to shore and see if we can get a better view from there."

She swivelled round and glared at me, her beetroot-stalk topknot now wet and limp over her face. "Hold my legs, you wee bampot!"

I didn't know what a **bampot** was, but I suspected it wasn't very flattering. I took a moment to decide whether it would be worse for me to be eyeball to eyeball with a loch monster or eyeball to eyeball with an angry Murdy.

For some reason, Murdy seemed the more terrifying prospect, so when she said, "Just do it, Benji," I did what I was told and held on to her legs.

"Go on then, stick your face in. See if you can see it."

"Don't let go," she said to me very sternly. "Okay, here goes—" But just as she tried to plunge her head into the water, the back end of the boat suddenly rose up really high into the air, like the top end of a see-saw. Mr Dog tried to stop himself with his paws, but he slid all the way down to the front. I couldn't stay upright

and fell on my face and Murdy flapped her arms about shouting, "What did you just go and do?" like she was accusing me of possessing special boat-lifting powers.

We were raised up in the air like that for a good few seconds, Mr Dog and I both whimpering and Murdy shouting at me to stop messing about, because she still had it in her head that I was responsible for the steep angle of the boat.

She was just yelling, "Put the boat back on the water, Benji!" when the boat slammed back onto the water with such force that we were catapulted into the loch. Which, considering the circumstances, felt like the last place I wanted to be.

Once I surfaced, I wanted to get back on the boat as soon as possible. Being in the water with a monster on the loose was not the most relaxing of situations and I thrashed about panicking for a bit, with my life jacket bobbing up under my armpits and in front of my face so I couldn't really see very well. It wasn't the most productive reaction.

Murdy must have thought the same thing about getting out of the loch sharpish, because she swam right over the top of me, then pushed down on my face to help heave herself onto the boat.

I tried as best I could to tread water, but I had my trainers on, and it is difficult to tread water in footwear. I was feeling more than a bit terrified, so I stuck my hand out for Murdy to help pull me back onto the boat, but she didn't take it.

"Oi, give me a hand," I shouted as best I could through mouthfuls of loch water.

But she just stood there, looking at me with those bulging eyes of hers.

I tried again, "Murdy, help me!"

Still she didn't respond. It was almost like she was frozen.

And then she pointed a shaky finger at the water.

I sensed it before I saw it. Something was right below me. Something big and dark and menacing. I looked down into the water and saw a shadow. A shadow that was growing...no, not growing, it was rising upwards from the depths of the loch. It was coming for me.

The Loch Lochy Monster.

I actually felt my whole body pulse in panic. "Quick! Murdy!" I shouted. "Pull me out!"

She didn't pull me out, instead she shouted, "What are you doing, Benji?"

Which really wasn't the reaction I was hoping for. Surely it was obvious what I was doing.

Mr Dog, who had managed to avoid falling in, put his face over the side of the boat and gave me a very forlorn look. Then he stuck his head into Murdy's side, like he  couldn't bear to watch what was about to happen.

This can't be how I die, I thought. Swallowed up by a monster in front of a poppy-eyed Scottish girl who was dressed like a beetroot. Even at my most visionary, I would never have imagined that. Stanley would be so mad at me if I'd got myself swallowed up by something he didn't think existed and I couldn't leave him completely on his own. But things weren't looking good, and I didn't know what to do. So I prayed to God and lords Brahma and Vishnu and, for some reason, Spider-Man. I don't know why, he just popped into my head, probably due to the terror.

I don't know which one of them answered my calls for help, but, out of nowhere, some type of superhuman aquatic strength must have been ignited deep inside me because, with one huge kick of my legs, I launched myself upwards towards the boat. I don't know how I did it, but I managed to grab onto the side and heave myself out of the water.

I lay gasping in a puddle at Murdy's feet while she stood over me saying, "What just happened, Benji? Seriously, what's going on?"

"Monster," I spluttered, "my monster – it's real!"

CHAPTER 13

A PEELY-WALLY BAHOOCHIE

Whether it was God or lords Brahma and Vishnu or even Spider-Man (although probably not Spider-Man – I'm not sure water is his thing), whoever had given me the strength to get myself out of the loch must have been feeling exceptionally obliging that day, because all of a sudden the waters became still.

The Loch Lochy Monster had vanished.

I waited for a moment, just to be certain – I've seen enough movies to know monsters have a tendency to suddenly leap out at you and gnaw off a limb, just when you think you're safe. But the loch remained calm, and the monster didn't return.

Lying on my front in a puddle, I thanked God and the lords and even Spider-Man for saving me, and by the time I had the strength to raise my head from the floor of the boat and speak, Murdy had stopped asking me to explain what had happened.

Instead, she had her hands over her eyes.

"Murdy, it's okay, it's gone."

I was a little confused when she shouted, "It's not the monster. It's that! Cover it up!"

"Cover what up?"

With one hand still over her face, she waved her other hand in my general direction. "That!"

"What?" I shouted again.

"That!"

It was then that I understood what she was talking about. When I'd pulled myself onto the boat my shorts and pants must have shot down to my ankles from the weight of the water and the sheer force of my excellent jump. I was lying face down on the floor of the boat with my bum fully on show. The only time I've pulled my pants up so quick was when one of Mum's friends accidentally burst into the toilet at home when I was sitting down for a relaxing poo with a copy of *The Beano*.

"Is it gone?" she said.

"Yes, it's gone."

She dropped her hands away from her face and in a quiet and slightly scary voice she said, "Never, ever, allow your PEELY-WALLY BAHOOCHIE out again. Do you understand?"

"Not really. What's a peely-wally bahoochie?"

"Your wee pale bum! I don't ever want to see it, got it?" she said very ferociously.

I gulped and then I nodded. "I understand. I'm sorry about that."

I thought my apology might have eased the tension, but then she jabbed her finger within a centimetre of my nose and started shouting, "I told you to get hold of my legs!" which I genuinely think was both unfair and uncalled for.

And I was not having her jabbing her finger at me, so I let my finger do some jabbing of its own and shouted back at her. "I had hold of your legs. You bampot!"

I hoped I'd used that insult correctly. I think I did because she did not look happy – her whole face crumpled in on itself.

"If you had hold of my legs, how did I fall in?"

"I was still holding on to your legs when *we* fell in! It wasn't the leg-holding that was the problem, I was doing a brilliant job of leg-holding –" I pointed out at the water – "it was the humungous monster out there that was the problem."

"The monster out there..." She said the words like she had forgotten the teeny tiny detail of the Loch Lochy Monster. Her face stopped looking quite so angry and she took her finger away from my nose and took a breath. "You may be right." She looked out across the water. "Did you see it from where you were? What did it look like?"

I drew back my own finger and shook my head. "No, I didn't see it – not properly enough to describe it, other than being big and dark. But I felt it."

She gasped. "It touched you? Where?"

"It didn't touch me physically. I meant I felt its presence."

"Oh," she said flatly.

I said, "I think we all felt its presence, didn't we, Mr Dog? It was a mighty big presence."

Mr Dog came out from under the seat, nodded his head and let out a teeny whimper.

"I sort of saw it," Murdy went on. "Well, its shadow… right under you…maybe."

I gulped. "I bet it looked massive from where you were."

"Honestly, I thought you were a goner, for sure."

I shivered at the thought that moments earlier I had been swimming above a ginormous loch monster. I quickly thanked God, the lords and Spider-Man again, so they knew just how grateful I was.

Murdy gave me a very strange look and said, "What was *that* about?"

"Just thanking my possible protectors – you know, God and the Hindu lords Brahma and Vishnu…and Spider-Man." Explaining it to Murdy made me feel a little bit daft.

"*Spider-Man* is your protector?"

"I don't know that he's not."

"You're a strange one, Benji. But if it's protection you're after, you should add Guanyin to your list. She's the Chinese goddess of mercy and compassion and she is also the patron saint of sailors and fishermen."

"Thanks, Murdy. She does sound like someone I'd want in my corner. She's on the list. I wish I'd known about her earlier."

Murdy nodded in quite a satisfied way, and I nodded back, grateful she had made me feel a little less daft. She picked up an oar and sat herself down in her rowing position, then she shook her head and said, "Well, that was fun."

"Fun?" Clearly, she had a totally different idea about fun to me. I don't have a complete fear of the water, like Stanley does, but I know all too well that sometimes it is not a safe place to be. Especially with a monster about.

"Yeah, it was quite the performance. You have completely convinced me there is a Loch Lochy Monster."

I was a bit surprised by that comment. "I thought you were already convinced. You said you'd seen it before."

She looked across the water. "You realize no one

else will believe it exists?"

"Well, we've both seen it, so it must. And soon everyone else will believe it exists too and the tourists will come in their droves and Uncle Hamish won't have to leave."

And Stanley will believe me too, I thought.

Murdy scrunched up her nose. "How did you work that one out?"

"Duh – we've got proof now – two eyewitness accounts—"

Mr Dog barked.

"Sorry, I mean three eyewitness accounts."

"Nice idea, but if you think people round here are going to believe two kids banging on about a loch monster, you're even more of a bampot than you look. Believe me, I know, and I'm not going through all that again."

"I've got it!" I said, leaping to my feet and making the boat rock. I didn't fancy another dip in the water, so I sat back down carefully (but also quickly) and tried to control my excitement. "What we need is proof! Actual physical evidence. A photo or a video or, even better, a Loch Lochy Monster tooth!"

Murdy raised one eyebrow. "You think you can get a loch monster's tooth? Not likely!"

"Okay, maybe not a tooth, but we could try and get some photo or video evidence, don't you think?"

"It's a nice idea, but how are you going to do that? I can't imagine the Loch Lochy Monster is one for taking a selfie."

Obviously, I wasn't expecting the Loch Lochy Monster to provide us with a selfie. "I am one hundred per cent positive that *we* can get a photo of the Loch Lochy Monster. All we have to do is hunt it down. We've seen it once, we're bound to see it again," I said, albeit very wrongly as it turned out.

"Hmmm. Maybe... If we had something that looked like evidence, everyone who called me a liar would have to eat their words. Kay McGavin, Clarissa and Camilla would have to take back what they said about me." She looked back at Loch Lochy. It was incredible how calm the waters were, considering what had just happened. "You're not too scared to come out here again?"

I was a little frightened...okay, a lot frightened, but then I thought of Dad's name carved into his tree, and my fear gave way to determination. Loch Lochy Holiday Lets belonged to the McLaughlins. I would not just stand by and watch it being taken away.

"No, I'm not too scared. Are you?"

"No! Murdy Mei-Yin McGurdy doesn't do fear!" She flicked her head and her damp ponytail spun about like a helicopter blade.

I didn't know what to comment on first, the name thing or the hair thing. I went with the name thing. "Your name is Murdy McGurdy? Murdy McGurdy? No, you're having me on."

"What's wrong with Murdy McGurdy?"

I didn't want to answer that, so I decided it was best to move on. "It's a deal then? We'll come back tomorrow and get some hard concrete evidence that the Loch Lochy Monster exists."

"The hardest concretiest evidence there is," Murdy said, and Mr Dog gave a little WOOF to show he was on board with my excellent plan too.

Well, I say woof, it was more of a whimpery whine, like he wasn't one hundred per cent convinced by my spectacular vision, but I was sure I'd win him over.

CHAPTER 14

AN ACCIDENTAL GIFT OF AWESOME

While we were mooring the boat, Murdy told me that it would probably be best if we didn't rush in and tell everybody about what had happened.

"You're right, Murdy," I said, "we need to wait until we have the evidence. Grown-ups have trouble believing things unless they see them for themselves."

She pulled a face. "I've experienced first-hand how people react when you start talking about monsters. You don't need to tell me I'm right. I know I'm right. I'm right about most things. You'd do well to remember that, Benji McLaughlin."

Back at the house, we found Clara and Uncle Hamish having another serious conversation, which they stopped as soon as they saw us. They were obviously talking about Gregor McGavin, and I wanted to tell Uncle Hamish right there and then that he shouldn't worry, I was on it and that I had a fail-safe monster plan.

He looked me up and down, his eyes stopping at the wet footprints I'd made on the kitchen floor. "Did you go for a swim in your clothes, laddie?"

In all the excitement of my visionary plan-making, I'd forgotten Murdy and I were still pretty damp. "We did indeed go for a swim in our clothes," I said, because they wouldn't believe me if I told them that we'd been knocked overboard by the Loch Lochy Monster. Not just yet anyway.

"Oh, Murdy Mei-Yin McGurdy! Give me strength!" Clara said, slapping her hand to her forehead. "Why did you do a thing like that? I didn't bring you anything to change into."

"It's not a problem," Uncle Hamish said, "she can borrow something of Benji's. They're about the same size."

"I'm taller, actually," Murdy and I said at the same time.

I wasn't sure how I felt about lending her some of my clothes. I didn't have that many because we could only bring one suitcase on the train up from London. The rest of Stanley and my things were being sent up later. I thought I'd be annoyed about not having all my stuff, but I wasn't. It's people you miss. Not things.

Anyway, I was busy thinking about whether I would be prepared to part with one of my few outfits, when Murdy said, "I'm not wearing anything of *his*. I might catch something English off them and besides, they'll probably be too small."

That made my mind up immediately. If she didn't want to, I *really wanted* her to wear my clothes.

"I'll get changed up in my room and then bring you some down."

"That's very kind of you, Benji. Isn't that kind, Murdy?" Clara put her hands on her hips and gave Murdy a strong look which suggested that Murdy should confirm that I was.

Murdy, however, mumbled something which, to me,

did not sound very confirmatory at all.

Upstairs, Stanley was lying on his bed with his headphones in. He took one earbud out when he saw me. "Why are you wet?"

"We got knocked off the boat by the Loch Lochy Monster. If you'd stayed around you would have seen it."

Stanley rolled his eyes. "The Loch Lochy Monster? Give over, Benji. Do you always have to be such a child?"

I didn't know how to answer, what with me being an actual child.

"And can you *not* mess about on the water?"

"But there was a monster, Stanley! A huge one!"

"Just don't." Stanley gave me a look somewhere between disappointment and annoyance, then stuck his earbud back in.

I was expecting him to be a little more excited – I'd seen an actual loch monster, well, sort of! But never mind, he'd have to believe me when Murdy and I showed him hard concrete evidence of the concretiest kind.

I grabbed a pair of shorts, a T-shirt and some socks from my drawer. I drew the line at underpants. There was no way I was lending her a pair of my boxers.

When I handed them over to Murdy, Clara said, "What do you say?"

Murdy said, "Thank you," even though she didn't look like she wanted to, then she went off to the downstairs loo to change.

When she came back out, she grinned at me and said, "I reckon this T-shirt probably suits me better, don't you think so?"

I did NOT think so. I'd only gone and given her my T-shirt that had the slogan on it, **The Owner of this T-shirt is Awesome**. "I am the *owner* of that T-shirt; you are only the borrower."

She cupped her hand to her ear. "Sorry, did you say something? I can't hear you. I'm too busy over here being **awesome** in my **awesome** T-shirt."

I cupped my own hand over my ear and said, "I'm sorry, I can't hear you because I'm surrounded by a cloud of invisible awesomeness that doesn't let the voices of unawesome people through."

Uncle Hamish rolled his eyes. "Nice to see you two kids getting along."

Clara drained the last of her coffee and put the cup in the sink. "Come on, Murdy, let's get you home, we've taken up enough of these good people's time." Then she touched Uncle Hamish's arm and said, "I'll go over the numbers again, but I can't see any other way. I reckon you've got three to four weeks max."

"What do you mean three to four weeks?" I said.

Uncle Hamish ruffled my hair. "Och, nowt for you to be concerned about. And nowt your old uncle can't sort."

I looked up at him and gave him my *you're not fooling me look* – it was obvious they were talking about how long he had until we lost everything to the McGavins – but he did not seem to notice.

Instead, he turned to Clara and nodded. "I appreciate your help, I really do."

She smiled. "I know, Hamish."

Murdy and I both curled our noses up at Uncle Hamish and Clara being so obviously nice to each other. No one needs to see that.

As Murdy left, she turned to me and said, "Say goodbye to awesome."

"I can hardly say goodbye to myself, can I?"

Then, in a rather unfriendly voice, she said, "I'll come tomorrow, shall I? Not to see you, but for that thing we were going to do, you know, the *project*?"

"Yeah, fine, come if you want, but only for the *project*," I said, in an equally unfriendly voice.

After they'd gone, I realized Uncle Hamish was

looking at me. "What?" I said, a little crossly.

"You two seemed to hit it off well."

"She is one of the rudest people I have ever met. Are all Scottish kids like that?"

Uncle Hamish walked to the kitchen cupboard and offered me a Penguin. The chocolate biscuit type, not the Antarctic bird type. "She's always seemed very sweet to me."

I unwrapped the bar and stared at him before I took a bite. He had to be joking. Murdy...*sweet*?

I mustn't have looked convinced because Uncle Hamish said, "They're good people, the McGurdys."

I suppose Murdy hadn't laughed at me when I told her about my protectors. In fact, she'd given me the goddess Guanyin. "She seems *alright*," I conceded.

Uncle Hamish smiled this knowing smile, like he always knew Murdy and I would get on. "And what's this project *thing* you two are up to tomorrow?"

I grinned back at him. "It is a completely excellent plan but top secret, so I can't tell you what it's about – not yet. But when I can, you, Uncle Hamish, are going to be umazed with a capital U!"

"You know you spell *amazed* with an A not a U, don't you?"

"Yes, I do."

I did not. Let's say I've always been a bit of an imaginative speller.

Bedtime prayers took a little longer that night, because I had to add Spider-Man into the mix, just in case he *had* played a part in saving Mr Dog, Murdy and me from being gobbled up by the Loch Lochy Monster. I also added the Chinese goddess Guanyin, because I liked the sound of her. When I got to the part where I said, "Wherever they are, please keep Mum and Dad safe and help them to get back to us—" something hit me in the back. I was interrupted before I had even managed the amens and awomens (again – who really knows – best to cover all bases).

Stanley shouted, "Oh shut up, Benji. Just shut up!"

I jumped up from my kneeling position and found Stanley's paperback copy of *Engineering in the 21st Century* lying next to me. "What did you do that for, bumface?"

Unhelpfully, Mr Dog thought he was in the middle of

a game of fetch, because he returned Stanley's missile to him. Stanley then said, "Who are you calling bumface? Bumface!" then launched it at me again. This time he missed.

"Stop it, Stanley! Why did you interrupt me right in the middle of my praying ritual?"

"Because it's stupid."

"It's not stupid. You just lack vision."

"It is stupid. And I have enough vision to know that praying to Spider-Man is not going to make a difference."

"It might."

"It won't."

"You can't know that for certain."

"I can, Benji. Because—" He hesitated.

"Because?"

The anger drained out of his voice, and he spoke so quietly I almost couldn't hear him. "Because they're dead, Benji. Mum and Dad are dead. And every time I have to remind you of that, it's like I'm killing them all over again."

I didn't ask what he meant at the time when he said

145

killing them, because I was too cross at him. I wish I had. I might have been able to help him sooner.

He then said, "I'm worried about you, Benji," which surprised the crossness out of me because, clearly, he was the one to worry about. "I'm worried that you're not dealing with things very well."

This also surprised me. I was dealing with things perfectly well. Way better than him. He was the one chucking books about. And being an eternal grump. He was the one who had given up. Not me.

"It is okay, you know – to be sad," he continued. "It's not good to bottle things up."

"You're one to talk! Who do you speak to?"

Stanley said very quietly, "I spoke to my counsellor. I might probably speak to one here too."

"Well, I already won at counselling. I don't need it any more."

"You don't *win* at counselling, Benji! And certainly not by telling people what you think they want to hear."

I know now he was trying to be kind, but at the time he just annoyed me because he was telling me stuff that I thought I already knew. I thought I was coping with the sadness just fine.

"I am sad, Stanley. I am sad that Mum and Dad aren't here. I am sad that you're so sad. I am sad about how much I miss them. But I won't ever let the sadness win. And I won't ever be sad that they're dead when they're not."

Stanley sighed. "Okay, Benji. You carry on."

He crawled back into his bed, and I knelt down next to mine and began praying again, but this time much louder, so he'd have to listen.

When I finally got under my duvet, with Mr Dog lying over my feet like a doggy hot-water bottle, my mind whirled all over the place. I tried to direct my thoughts to be angry ones about Stanley, but I couldn't. Because hiding beneath my manufactured anger, my real feelings were throbbing. Big, overwhelming emotions that I couldn't look at directly. The deep gnawing sadness that comes with missing someone.

I closed my eyes tight to squeeze the thoughts away.

And I saw it.

The dark shadow of the Loch Lochy Monster circling below me.

CHAPTER 15

MURDY, THE PICKPOCKET

Stanley was still sleeping when I woke up the following morning – his face twisted into a frown. At first, I thought *How very Stanley to be able to be grumpy even when he's asleep*, but then I realized that he was probably having another bad dream. I went over and put my hand on his shoulder and whispered, "It's okay, Stan."

His eyes flickered open, he saw it was me, said, "Benji," and his face relaxed.

"Get a bit more sleep, if you need it," I said.

He did a little nod, then turned over and drifted off again.

By the time I went down for breakfast, Murdy was already sat in my chair at the table eating a bowl of Cookie Crumbles, with Mr Dog at her feet. She was still wearing MY awesome T-shirt.

"Mum never lets me have these," she was saying to Uncle Hamish as she shovelled some more in her mouth.

He looked worried for a second, then said, "Well maybe don't tell her I let you then."

I sat down next to her and poured myself a bowl. "That's my T-shirt."

She grinned at me. "Are you sure?"

"Yes! I lent it to you yesterday."

"I only ask because it says the owner is someone awesome."

"I know! Me!"

Uncle Hamish laughed and ruffled my hair. "Murdy's teasing you, laddie. And it's nay bother for you to lend her a T-shirt."

I wasn't so sure about that. Her wearing it was surely breaking the Trade Descriptions Act because my T-shirt was definitely not describing her.

When he disappeared into his office, Murdy pointed the end of her spoon at me. "I've been thinking. Have you got something to film the Loch Lochy Monster with?"

"I kind of hoped you might have."

She shook her head. "You don't have a phone or anything?"

"No."

"What about your brother?"

"There's no way Stanley's going to let me borrow his phone."

"We'll just have to take it then, when he's not looking."

I wasn't sure about that. "He'd go mad at me if he found out."

"Not when we show him the Loch Lochy Monster, he won't."

"I don't even know how I'd get it. He carries it around with him everywhere."

"Don't worry, leave it to me. I'll distract him and then swipe it when he's not looking."

I couldn't imagine anyone being able to swipe

anything from Stanley. "I don't think that will work somehow."

"Trust me. I'm very good at pickpocketing," Murdy said proudly. "I was the Artful Dodger in our school production of *Oliver* – I practised it a lot to help me get into the role."

Murdy did strike me as someone who might have secret criminal tendencies – she seemed the wily sort, but still, I wasn't sure an unlawful approach was the best idea. "I dunno. I could just ask him – he might say yes?"

"You think so?"

I could tell she didn't think so and, if I was being honest, I didn't think so either. "Probably not."

"Right, we'll go with *my* plan then. You go down and get the boat in the water—"

"Me to the water?"

"Er, yes, that's where the wee water beastie will be. You're not scared, are you?"

In truth, I was scared. But maybe the most important adventures are scary, and you just have to have them anyway. I had to ignore the fear and focus on finding

151

my monster, so I could save the McLaughlin family home from Gregor McGavin. And also, so I could show Stanley that it was okay to believe in the impossible.

"No, I'm not scared," I said, because I wasn't about to go into all that detail with Murdy.

"Good. Me neither. So, you and Mr Dog head to the boat, and I'll get the phone. And don't worry, I'll be very subtle about it. Trust me. Mrs McAllister said I was the most convincing Artful Dodger she had ever seen."

I don't think Mrs McAllister could have seen many Artful Dodgers and I don't think Murdy could have been very subtle in her robbery, because three minutes after Mr Dog and I had got the boat into the water, I heard a shout of, "Get the oars and GET READY!" and then a furious shout of, "Give me back my phone, you little Scottish thief." And then I saw Murdy tearing down the path and Stanley chasing her in his pyjamas.

Mr Dog looked up at me and I swear he shook his head in a way that made me think that this was exactly how he'd expected Murdy's plan to unfold.

Luckily, what Murdy lacked in subtlety she made up for in speed, and as Stanley didn't have anything on his feet, he had to slow down when he reached the gravel path. When Murdy reached the shore, she dived face first into the boat, grabbed an oar and shouted, "Look lively, get paddling, noodle-arms!"

Stanley started shouting at me, "Benji, you bring my phone back this instant, or you'll live to regret it!"

"I can't, Stanley," I hollered back as I started to plunge the oars into the water, "it's for a good cause, you'll see!"

Even though we had been rowing frantically, Murdy and I hadn't quite got into our rhythm. We weren't that far out by the time Stanley reached the water, but I could tell he wasn't prepared to come in after us.

"I swear to God, Benji, if you don't bring it to me now, I will punish you so badly."

"You don't believe in God, remember? Besides, I think God would be on my side about this. And so would lords Brahma and Vishnu and Guanyin and probably Spider-Man too."

"What are you talking about?" Stanley's face had gone quite an angry red colour and I was pleased that we were rowing further and further away from him.

"I'll give it back to you soon, Stanley, I promise. I wouldn't be doing this if it wasn't absolutely necessary. You have to believe me."

Stanley cupped his hands round his mouth and shouted, "I don't have to believe anything, Benji. Now turn round and bring it back, RIGHT NOW!"

I pretended I couldn't hear him. "Okay, Stanley. That's great. We'll bring it back soonish."

"Bring it back now, I said!"

"Okay, in an hour or two. Thanks! You're the best!"

"Benjiiiiii!"

I dug my oar in a bit quicker! I'd have deal with the wrath of Stanley later, but right then, I was focused on our monster mission. "Keep rowing, Murdy."

"What does it look like I'm doing, flying a kite?"

It didn't look like that at all, so I reckoned she must have been being sarcastic. I was feeling quite pleased with myself, because I had definitely made huge improvements in my paddling technique from the day before – no way Murdy could call my arms noodly now. Although, when I said that she responded by saying, "Aye, you're doing a fine job...Mr Noodle-arms," as though the Mr made a difference!

Once we were far enough away not to hear Stanley shouting at us, we had a break from our paddling to discuss the plan of action. But as soon as we came to a stop, Mr Dog jumped straight into the water and began paddling about. Mr Dog is clearly a very brave dog. He didn't even hesitate to get in the water, despite having seen the Loch Lochy Monster there the day before. I wished I was as courageous as him. I have to admit,

155

I felt a little sicky-nervous when the possibility of being knocked in again crossed my mind.

"There's no monster here," Murdy said. "Let's head back to where you saw it yesterday."

I felt relieved that there was no monster in the immediate vicinity, even though I knew that the whole point of us being out on the water was to track it down. "You're right, it can't be near here if Mr Dog is happy to go in."

Heading back to where we'd been the day before seemed like a good idea, although neither of us could agree on where exactly we'd been the day before.

"It was definitely more over that way," I told Murdy.

"That way – very precise. And you're wrong." She pointed her oar in completely the opposite direction. "We were over there in between those white and orange buoys."

I had a very strong feeling that she was the one who was wrong, because I hadn't seen any buoys the day before. I put my oar down, closed my eyes and concentrated.

"What are you doing now?" Murdy asked.

156

"I'm trying to see if I can sense where the Loch Lochy Monster is. You know, pick up on its presence."

"You're a pure skyrocket, man."

"What's a – oh, never mind. Now, can you be quiet? I need complete silence for monster sensing."

I waited for a few minutes to see if I could pick up on anything, but I wasn't getting a clear idea as to the monster's whereabouts, *at all*. When I opened my eyes, Murdy had her arms crossed and she and Mr Dog were looking at me with very unimpressed expressions. "Sense anything?"

"No, not really."

"Shocker!" she said. "Look, we could row about with Mr Dog up on the helm. If he's really the one who can detect the monster, like you say he can, he'll start growling again if we're close."

"That, Murdy McGurdy, is an awesome idea."

It turned out it wasn't that awesome, because we spent the next two hours rowing aimlessly around the lake, hoping Mr Dog's doggy nose would pick up on the Loch Lochy Monster. There was *one* exciting moment when Mr Dog started growling at a dark shape floating in the water. Cautiously we rowed up to it, and I prayed we weren't willingly approaching certain doom, but it turned out to be a tree branch. Apart from that, we found nothing monstery, *at all.*

Eventually, because my arms were beginning to hurt and my bum was beginning to ache and I really needed a wee and something to eat, I called an end to the search. "This is so disappointing. It's not here. I've annoyed Stanley for nothing."

"It seems that way," Murdy said. "Are you sure you don't sense it around anywhere?"

"I don't think it wants to be found today. Maybe we'll find it tomorrow." As the words passed my lips, a worrying thought struck me, and I felt myself sink in the middle.

Murdy must have noticed because she said, "What's up? Your face looks like a haggis that's been dropped on the floor."

"What if that's it?" I said, choosing to ignore her haggis comment. "What if we don't find it before Uncle Hamish is forced to sell? From what your mum said yesterday, we've only got three weeks – four maximum!"

"I did tell you it wouldn't be easy to get a photo of it. We've only been looking for two hours. Who knows if you'll see it again."

"Remind me, when did you last see it?"

I didn't know why, but Murdy blushed a little. "Er, I suppose about two years ago. Give or take."

I could hear the panic in my voice when I said – okay, screamed – "What if it takes years before it comes back? What then?"

She shrugged. "I don't know."

Astonishingly, it was beginning to look like my remarkable and visionary Loch Lochy Monster plan might have one or two flaws.

"I'm sure we'll spot it again soon," I said, more confidently. "You have to be positive about these things."

Murdy nodded. "Aye, you do."

But after a few more days of thorough Loch Lochy searching and no sign of the Loch Lochy Monster, my confidence and positivity were suffering badly. At night I lay in bed looking at the stars through the gap in the curtains, worrying that we really would lose our little part of Loch Lochy – and the house and the cabins and even Dad's special tree – to Gregor McGavin. And that Mum and Dad wouldn't know where to find us when they came back and all those were thoughts I just couldn't bear.

CHAPTER 16

TROUBLE ON ROLLER SKATES

When your confidence and positivity have taken a battering, it is time to take stock and reassess. Murdy had found her da's old camera, so we hadn't had to risk the wrath of Stanley by trying to nick his phone again. But all we'd managed to capture were a few fuzzy photos of floating bits of wood, a plastic bag and a video of a disinterested-looking heron. All very **unmonstery**. With this in mind, the morning after our eighth unsuccessful attempt at monster spotting, I called an emergency meeting with Murdy. Time was really against us. Worst case scenario, Gregor McGavin would want his money back in two more weeks. Uncle

Hamish *might* be able to put him off a bit longer – he was Uncle Hamish after all, and I'd seen him handle Gregor McGavin before – but we also had the start of school to consider. We could not, in my opinion, spend any more time drifting about on the water trying to spot the Loch Lochy Monster. We needed to be proactive.

We met down at the park, where we took it in turns to push Mr Dog in the baby swing. Which he enjoyed immensely. When he flew forward his flappy ears would stream out behind and when he swung back, they'd cover his face like furry curtains.

"The hunting of the Loch Lochy Monster is not going brilliantly," I said.

"That is a fair assessment of the situation," Murdy said.

"I wonder what it's up to. Why it shows up, then disappears," I said.

"I really don't know."

"Who does know the thought processes of a loch monster?" I sighed. "Anyway, with time against us, I no longer think we can continue with this plan." I quite liked how official I was sounding.

"Do you have another idea?" Murdy asked.

"Yes, I do."

"And are you going to share it with me?"

"I am. Are you ready?"

"Aye, crack on," Murdy said, with a little less enthusiasm than I would have liked.

"My brother Stanley reckons you shouldn't believe anything without evidence."

"I know, but we haven't been able to get any evidence and you can't just conjure up a Loch Lochy Monster out of nowhere." She did a big, and very unnecessary eye-roll when she said that.

"Oh, can't you?" I said that very mysteriously, to really get her interested and stop all the eye-rolling.

It worked, because she said, "Go on..." in a very interested-sounding voice.

"We need to make our own evidence." I took a step forward and did a big dramatic gesture with my hands. "We'll create our own monster."

I waited for her to gasp in wonder at my fantastic idea, but she didn't. She just said, "What a live one, like Frankenstein?" which sort of piddled on my parade.

"What? No!" What a thing to say. "We're not going to make a *live* one. We'll make something that looks like a loch monster and show people pictures of that."

"Isn't that fraud?"

"I wouldn't say it would be fraud as such. The Loch Lochy Monster definitely exists. It's just shy. Sometimes." I knew Murdy had a point, but I was desperate. I didn't like the thought of having to deceive people, but I *had* seen a monster, so I told myself it wouldn't be classed as a bad lie. It was one of those white ones that you tell for the greater good, like when Mum would get a dodgy haircut and I'd tell her she looked magnificent. Or when Dad cooked an inedible meal and I'd tell him it was restaurant-worthy.

"I don't have a problem with committing fraud," Murdy said very casually and in a way that suggested she might have done it before. "Everyone thinks I'm a liar anyway."

"I really don't think it would be fraud."

"Don't worry, we're kids, we'll get off any charges. They'll call it misadventure and say we were being high-spirited."

I stared at her. It really did sound like she had some first-hand experience. "There won't be any charges."

"Of course – none that will stick anyway."

Talking about breaking the law was starting to make me feel nervous. "Can we please think about how we can make a fake, yet extremely convincing, Loch Lochy Monster?"

"Aye, absolutely." Murdy rubbed her chin and looked thoughtful. "Now what can we make a loch monster out of...you know, there's a whole load of stuff in the shed at home that we could have a look through. Although I'm not quite sure how we could turn it into a fake, yet extremely convincing Loch Lochy Monster."

We fell silent for a while to let our brains consider my plan, but we were rudely interrupted by a group of girls on roller skates. The three of them came pelting round the corner and screeched to a stop outside the park gate. I might be misremembering things, but I think they were cackling in a very unnerving way. They reminded me a bit of those monkeys on wheels in that film called *Return to Oz*. Screechy and a bit scary-looking. But with less fur and more denim and sequins.

And so tall, all three of them practically giants.

Murdy whispered, "It's Kay and the twins. Just try and be cool," in a slightly anxious way that made me think she thought I was the least cool person on the planet. Then she said, in one of those voices that sounded fake-relaxed and therefore try-hard and not at all cool, "Hey, Kay. Hey, Clarissa, Camilla."

The dark-haired girl in the middle with beady black eyes, who I guessed was Kay McGavin because she shared certain bird-like qualities with her dad,

(although if he was a pigeon, her height would make her an ostrich), did a very sneery face and said, "Are you seriously pushing a dog in a swing like it's a baby?"

The twins laughed way too much. I'd never seen such enormous mouths. Their heads practically flipped backwards like pedal bins. Poor Mr Dog looked very embarrassed and tried to scramble out of the swing-seat, but he got in a right old tangle.

Either Clarissa or Camilla stuck her blonde plait in her mouth and began lazily chewing on it, looking me up and down while I tried to pull Mr Dog's leg free from where he'd got it stuck.

The other twin said, "Seen any monsters today, Murdy?" then stuck her plait in her mouth and had a good chomp on it too.

"Yeah, told any more whoppers?" Kay looked at me. "I'd watch her if I was you. Doesn't know how to tell the truth."

I thought Murdy would explode with rage, but she didn't. She just stood there, looking a bit sick. When I mouthed, "Are you alright?" she wouldn't look me in the eye.

Kay McGavin however, stared me right in the eyeballs and said, "So, tell me, what kind of weirdo pushes their dog in a swing?" She said the word weirdo as slowly and forcefully as possible, just in case I was in any doubt as to how weird she thought I was.

"He likes it," I said, trying to pull him out, though he was well and truly wedged in.

"He doesn't look like he likes it."

"You love it, don't you, Mr Dog?" Mr Dog looked at me like I had to be kidding.

Kay McGavin did this big splutter laugh. "You call your dog *Mr Dog*? Wow. Just wow!"

I did not appreciate all the negativity being directed towards me or Mr Dog and I was not about to be intimidated by an ostrich in sequins, so I said, "I'm sorry, who are you?" even though I knew exactly who she was.

She puffed up her chest and said, "I'm Kay McGavin," in a very hoity-toity voice.

I smiled. "Sorry, am I supposed to know you?"

"If you don't, you soon will," she said and even though I didn't think it was possible, her face got even more sneery. "But I know you. You're one of the English staying at that loser's place. My dad told me about you – you might know him, Gregor McGavin?"

That really made my elbows itch. "My uncle Hamish isn't a loser."

"That's not what my dad says," Kay said in a tinkly voice. Then she pushed off and started skating away backwards. Even though she was clearly EVIL, it was hard not to be impressed by her rollering skill.

She spun round in a circle, then set her sights on Murdy. "My dad knows a loser when he sees one. And so do I, isn't that right, Little Miss Liar-Pants?"

Kay and the massive-mouthed twins laughed again, then they skated off at high speed, only slowing down when they had to stomp across the grass, which totally ruined their dramatic exit.

I wondered if Murdy hadn't picked up on the fact that Kay had called her a liar and a loser. She hadn't stood up to her, which seemed very unlike the Murdy I had got to know. The Murdy I knew would have told them to go away and boil their heads.

I gave her a nudge. "They were delightful. What's the story with you and them?"

Murdy pursed her lips. "No story. I used to hang out with them a bit. Then they decided they didn't want to any more. Don't really know why. Then when my story about the Loch Lochy Monster came out, they got really mean."

"Doesn't sound like they'd be very good friends," I said.

"Guess not." After a bit of a struggle, she managed

to pull Mr Dog out of the swing. "Let's get going. We've got a loch monster to build. We're going to make our evidence, Benji McLaughlin, and I'll shut that lot up once and for all."

She may not have had the same noble motivation for monster building as me, but I was pleased Murdy was so energized about my new plan. No way were the McGavins going to get their hands or their roller skates on Uncle Hamish's land.

CHAPTER 17

IMPRINTS OF THE PAST

Mr Dog and I followed Murdy back to her house, which was a shortish walk down the lane. It was set back from the lake and higher up on the hill. From the path you might not have known it was even there – I only just spotted the off-white brick hidden among the tall evergreen trees.

"This is nice," I said, closing the squeaky garden gate behind me.

Murdy shrugged. "I guess. Mum is always moaning about the garden. Dad used to be in charge of that."

The garden was pretty wild, jungly even. The flowers which climbed up the front of the house looked like they were threatening to take the place over.

"After Dad left, Mum talked a bit about moving us to Hong Kong. My aunt Polly moved there and when Por Por and Gung Gung passed away, Mum wanted to be nearer her sister, but I didn't want to leave. I've only ever lived in Scotland and, despite what some people think, I can barely speak Cantonese. Besides, this is my home. In the end, I think she realized it was hers too. Even without Dad here."

"Well, I'm glad you stayed," I blurted out, which surprised us both.

I don't think Murdy knew how to respond because she thumped me on the arm. Not hard, I think it was just an instinctive reaction.

"Sorry," she said, eyes wide. "I don't know why I did that." Then she did a little giggle.

I stood there for a moment trying to figure out what had just happened, while Murdy busied herself tipping some broken flowerpots and an empty compost bag out from a garden trolley. She set off with a cry of, "Follow me!" and wheeled it along a little gravel path round to the back of the house. I followed her to a large run-down shed. She shoved the door open with her hip and pulled the light cord. Mr Dog padded about, sniffing around and pushing his nose into things he thought looked interesting. There was a lot for him to explore.

One end of the shed was packed full of junk. Fishing rods, tyres, a bag of shoes, a watering can with a hole in the bottom, several buckets, two rolls of faded carpet, an exercise bike, two mouldy-looking buoys, a surfboard, numerous cracked flowerpots, a long silver tumble-dryer hose, some sheets of metal, some old sacks and a load of other stuff.

"What is this place?"

"This is what Mum used to call my dad's man-cave."

"There's a lot of junk."

"Dad never liked to throw anything out. Used to drive Mum mad. Shame he wasn't as attached to people."

I did not quite know what to say to that. I wanted to say something supportive like, *You seem very attachable to me*, so she knew I felt bad for her, but I instead heard myself saying, "Oooh, is that a pogo stick back there?"

I don't know why. I suppose I panicked. Maybe I didn't want another thump. And I've always wanted a pogo stick.

Murdy didn't seem to mind my total lack of consideration. She gave herself a little shake and then got practical or, some might say, bossy. "Fill up the cart with whatever you think looks monstery."

I scanned over the jumble again. Nothing leaped out as being particularly monstery. I almost said something along those lines, but stopped when I realized those were the thoughts of a person with no vision. I would never be that person. I had to keep hoping and believing even when things didn't look great.

Especially when things didn't look great.

Murdy must have realized what I was thinking because she said, "I know it doesn't look like much now, but with little a bit of imagination I'm sure we can cobble a monster together from this lot."

"You're absolutely right," I said, although we wouldn't need a little bit of imagination. We would need *enormous* amounts of imagination to make a monster from the pile of rubbish we put in that cart.

Once it was full, we stood back and admired our collection of odds and ends. Mr Dog contributed a chewed welly and two grubby-looking tennis balls, which I thought had the potential to be Loch Lochy Monster eyes.

Then we carefully wheeled our haul back to Uncle Hamish's garage to get to work on the build. On our way back we walked past Stanley, who I was surprised to find painting the little picket fence outside Joan and Jacqueline. He was working at one end, Uncle Hamish at the other. They weren't talking, but there was a radio playing and Uncle Hamish was whistling along to a song I half recognized about a brown-eyed girl. It reminded me of Mum.

"What are you kids up to?" Uncle Hamish said when he saw us wheeling the cart down the path.

"Stuff," I said, because telling the truth would require far too much explanation.

"Stuff, hey?" Uncle Hamish smiled, leaned on the bit of fence he was painting, realized what he'd done, then slapped a hand to his forehead leaving a white palm print.

Even Stanley stopped painting to laugh.

Uncle Hamish shook his head and laughed at himself. "Well, you two have fun doing your stuff. Just don't do anything daft or dangerous."

"Course not," I said, then looked at Stanley. "You look like you're doing a good job there. Didn't have you down as a fence painter."

He shrugged and dipped his brush in the paint pot. "It's kind of relaxing."

Murdy and I left them to it and headed up to the garage. Uncle Hamish doesn't keep his Land Rover in the garage. He mainly uses it to store spare parts for all the holiday lets. There were four brand-new, if slightly dusty, toilets ready to go – I guess in case of a mass toilet emergency. I moved a cardboard box containing spare crockery from the workbench and put it down by the wall.

I was just standing up and saying to Murdy, "I think it's best if I sketch out what the Loch Lochy Monster might look like, so we know what to aim for," when something caught my eye.

Murdy must have noticed, because she said, "What's up?"

I pointed. "Look."

Murdy came over and stood next to me as I traced my fingers up the pen marks, some fainter than others.

Stuart aged 3 ½, 105 cm…aged 4, 106 cm…aged 4 ½, 111 cm…aged 5, 113 cm…aged 6, 120 cm…aged 7, 124 cm…aged 8, 130 cm…aged 9, aged 10, 149 cm…

*Hamish aged 3 ½, 108 cm...aged 4 ½, 114 cm...
aged 6, 122 cm...aged 6 ½, 129 cm...aged 7 ½, 138 cm...
aged 8, 146 cm...aged 9, 154 cm...aged 10, 161 cm...*

My eyes ran up and down the brickwork where my dad's and uncle's childhood had been marked. I imagined them standing there, heads pressed to the wall, necks stretched. I remembered Mum tickling me as Dad told me to hold still as he tried to measure me in our kitchen back at home, and Stanley laughing at how much taller he was than me.

I felt my chin wibble, but before the tears came, Murdy took me by the shoulders, turned me round and moved me so I was standing with my back against the wall. "Your dad's name is Stuart, right?"

I nodded.

She smiled and ran her hand across my head to the closest line. "*Stuart aged ten,*" she said. "Benji, you're exactly the same height!"

"I am?" I said and turned round to look.

"Yup, *exactly* the same height."

"He's imprinted into this place," I whispered as an overwhelming surge of desperation swept through me.

Our Loch Lochy Monster plan had to work. It just had to.

"Blimey, look at how tall Hamish was when he was thirteen!" Murdy said, pointing to a mark waaaay up the wall.

"That must have been when he cranked up his milk intake," I said.

Murdy frowned at me. "Okay…?"

I didn't explain what I meant. I didn't want her going home and drinking herself taller than me.

"Right, enough of this," I said giving myself a little shake out of the past and into the present. "We need to get this monster designed and crack on with building it."

I sketched out a picture of what I thought the Loch Lochy Monster might look like, which was a lot like the images I'd seen of the Loch Ness Monster – not the cartoon one with the tartan hat and bagpipes – but the fuzzy photo of it in the water.

Murdy looked at it and said, "It's hardly Leonardo da Vinci, but I get the idea."

"I think if we can create the general shape – a bit like a diplodocus – then cover it up with some sort of material and paint it dark green, we'll be good to go."

"What are you thinking dimensions-wise?"

I had thought about this already. "I do not think we should aim for a life-size model."

Murdy tilted her head and raised one eyebrow. "You think? I was all for creating a Loch Lochy Monster that would fill the garage."

"I think that might draw too much attention...oh, I see...you're joking. Okay, so I'm thinking we should aim for something just a little larger than two Mr Dogs. We can say it is a photo of the monster in the distance."

"Seems reasonable."

"I am very certain that we can pull this off," I said with all the confidence of someone who had absolutely no idea about how hard making a Loch Lochy Monster would be.

Murdy held up her hand. "High-five for friends who commit fraud together!"

I feel bad because I'd never usually do this, but I left her hanging. "I'm sorry, Murdy, committing fraud for a good reason is one thing, but high-fiving it seems a bit much."

She shrugged. "Suit yourself." Then she held up her hand for Mr Dog and he, with far fewer scruples than me, high-fived it with his paw.

Murdy and I spent most of the day fashioning a body out of an upturned flower planter, a cardboard box that had once contained a dishwasher and a couple of plastic buoys. The first problem we had was attaching the things together, which led to a row about whether Scotch tape or Sellotape was superior, or if they were, in fact, the same thing. It turned out it didn't really matter because neither of them worked.

We switched to some strong, thick black tape that we found in Uncle Hamish's toolbox. You know, the sort of stuff they use in movies to bind hostages' hands together. Although I'm sure that's not what Uncle Hamish uses it for. Surprisingly, it was working quite well and we had just managed to tape the buoys together, when Stanley walked in carrying two paintbrushes and a pot of paint.

Murdy hadn't noticed him and was in the middle of saying, "Do you think it's going to make the monster look a bit camel-y with those two humps for the body?"

Stanley put his brushes and pot down on a shelf and frowned a very deep frown. "You two have been hiding in here for ages. What are you up to? Why are you talking about camels? Why have you got those buoys taped together with gaffer tape?"

It was a lot to answer, and I knew I had to be at my most visionary to come up with something which would satisfy all his questions, without telling him the truth. It was a tall ask and, in the end, I opted for a diversionary tactic and said, "Would you like to have a go on Murdy's pogo stick?"

He studied my face for a moment before saying, "No, Benji, I would not like a go on Murdy's pogo stick. Uncle Hamish asked me to check on what you guys were up to. So what shall I tell him?"

"Tell him we're fine. That we are busy being...very creative."

Stanley rolled his eyes. "Whatever, Benji. I don't know what you're doing here, and I don't want to know, just don't bother me with anything ridiculous, okay?"

I was going to point out that it was him who had bothered me and ask when I had ever done anything ridiculous, but he left before I could say anything.

I watched him for a little while as he kicked up the stones on the path, his shoulders hunched over and his head down. He looked so lonely. So sad. I suppose that's what happens when you lose your hope. I wished I could run up to him and give him a hug and tell him things would be alright, but I thought he probably wouldn't want that.

I grabbed hold of the gaffer tape and began cutting off strips with new-found motivation. "Let's get on with this, Murdy. We'll show them. We'll make people believe in Loch Lochy Monsters. We'll save Uncle Hamish's home."

I looked back out at Stanley and then I said to myself, *I'll show you the unbelievable can happen, Stanley. I'll show you how to have hope again.*

I guess now I know that, deep down, I was probably trying to convince myself too. I know it might not make sense, but I thought if I could make people believe that the Loch Lochy Monster – something so improbable, something so implausible – was real, maybe I would also prove to myself that there was still a chance Mum and Dad would come home.

CHAPTER 18

OUR MONSTER MASTERPIECE (MAYBE)

Several rolls of gaffer tape, three arguments and two days later, our Loch Lochy Monster was complete. We were chuffed with the results.

We'd finished just after lunch and as we munched on some cheese and crisp sandwiches in the garage, I stood back to admire our creation and said, "Murdy, I do not want to sound boastful, but that monster is **MAGNIFICENT**."

Murdy said, spluttering out crumbs, "You are not being boastful, you are being honest. It is magnificent."

Looking back, I'm wondering if we'd lost some objectivity. We'd worked so hard and spent so many hours on it, we both thought it *must* be good. Or maybe the paint fumes had addled our brains because, with the benefit of hindsight, I can admit that our first monster model was not as convincing as we believed. Only Mr Dog looked at it with doubt in his bright doggy eyes, but I dismissed his opinion because I thought I was wiser than a dog. It turned out that I am not.

Very carefully, Murdy and I loaded our masterpiece onto the cart. Once we'd managed that, I said a prayer to God, lords Vishnu and Brahma and Guanyin and Spider-Man to bless our monster with good luck. Murdy huffed a lot while I was doing it and moaned that I was wasting time, but I really don't think you should overlook the importance of getting almighty beings on side.

Once I was done, the three of us headed down the slope to the loch to stage our photo, believing that, very soon, we'd have some excellent evidence and all Uncle Hamish's money worries would be over.

The monster model was quite heavy, so Murdy took hold of the handle at the front of the cart, and I pushed from the back. I definitely had the worse job because

I couldn't see past the monster's backside, and I kept tripping over the tail, which we'd made out of a tumble-dryer tube. As we hadn't allowed enough drying time, the bottoms of my legs were completely smeared with dark-green paint.

It was going to require a lot of patience and teamwork to get the monster down to the loch in one piece. Unfortunately, we didn't have much of either of those.

Murdy kept saying things like, "Are you actually helping or are you dangling off the back end and letting me do all the work?" and "Are you even pushing?" when I suspected she was the one not pulling.

We must have been right in the middle of arguing about who was the worst driver, because we didn't notice that Kay McGavin and the twins were sitting at the side of the path laughing at us. It was only when one of the tennis-ball eyeballs dropped off the monster and bounced off my head that we realized someone was lobbing stones at it. I stopped pushing and called out to Murdy to hold up so I could see what was going on. Mr Dog thought what was going on was a game of fetch and he chased after the tennis ball, caught it, then dropped it at my feet expecting me to throw it again, but it rolled back down the hill and into the loch.

Another stone hit the monster right in the body and tore through its cardboard-box middle, giving it an extra-large belly button. This annoyed me because I wasn't sure whether loch monsters had belly buttons, even of a regular size.

"Kay McGavin! Stop that!" I shouted. "You'll have someone's eye out."

Kay McGavin, however, did not seem to care about the dangers associated with rock-throwing and she chucked another stone. This one knocked the other eyeball off the monster, *exactly* like I predicted would happen. Mr Dog chased off down the hill after it, a happy smile on his face.

Kay waved her hand at our monster. "What is that even supposed to be? It looks like a green camel with a snout."

That was OUTRAGEOUS! It looked NOTHING like a green camel with a snout!

At the time, I thought our model was obviously a Loch Lochy Monster. Now I appreciate that it did not

bear as much resemblance to a Loch Lochy Monster as I'd thought. But this turned out to be a good thing, because if Kay McGavin and the twins had realized, they would have run their massive mouths off telling everybody about Murdy and me being fraudsters. But I wasn't thinking about that then, I was just very angry that Kay was being so rude about our magnificent monster, so I said, "What do you mean, *What's that supposed to be?* It's clearly a—"

Luckily, Murdy – who was trying her best to hide our monster behind her but failing spectacularly, because

she's nowhere near as tall as she thinks – did realize it would be best not to announce our plan. She nudged me in the ribs with her really pointy elbow and said to Kay, "*That* is none of your business."

Camilla and Clarissa gasped dramatically and looked at Kay to see how she was going to react. Kay stood up, looking impossibly tall. She took two giant steps forward, threw the rock she had in her hand up in the air and caught it again. "Say that again, Murdy McGurdy. I *dare* you."

I couldn't help it, I gulped very loudly. She was just

so threatening. Which was quite incredible considering she was wearing a LOT of sequins. I couldn't believe it when Murdy said, "*That* is none of your business," again!

This time it was the twins who gulped and me who gasped.

Kay took another step forward. "You're going to live to regret that!" she said. Then she threw her rock at our monster.

It knocked the mop-bucket-head clean off its body. I couldn't believe it. Our photographic evidence wouldn't be very convincing without a monstery head. I picked up the bucket and placed it under my arm, painting my armpit dark green in the process. Then I said, very slowly, my fury making my voice shake, "Look what you went and did!"

Kay either didn't care or didn't pick up on my anger because she said, "I don't know what I did because I don't know what that *thing* even is. What are you two weirdos up to?"

She did that thing where she said *weirdos* really slowly again, so we understood exactly how weird we were.

Murdy seemed to almost vibrate with rage when she said, also very slowly, "I told you, it's none of your business."

Kay's eyebrows shot together. "Everything is my business, I'm a McGavin and I demand that you tell me what that *thing* is."

Murdy took a step closer to Kay. "I'm Murdy Mei-Yin McGurdy and you can demand all you like, but I'm telling you, it's none of your business."

Kay took a step towards Murdy. "I know *exactly* who you are. And now you're going to get it!"

Murdy took another step forward and rose up on her tiptoes, so her eyes were about level with Kay's collarbone. "No, you're going to get it, McGavin."

Now, this is where it goes a little hazy. All the talk of *getting it* made me worried they were about to get into a proper fight. And that worried me because it might have meant *I* would have to get involved in a proper fight and I definitely did not want that to happen. I wanted to go and take pictures of our fake Loch Lochy Monster, not take a pummelling. I decided I had to do something to break them apart before any punches were thrown, so I said, "I think we're all getting a bit carried away and perhaps we all need to calm down."

Kay McGavin clutched her hands together, fake trembled and said, "*I think we're all getting a bit carried away and perhaps we all need to calm down,*" in a very whiney English-sounding voice.

Although Murdy herself had once taken the mickey out of my accent in a very similar way, she did not appear to like Kay doing it, so she shoved her. With both hands, right in the chest.

Kay swayed backwards, then swayed forward like a Weeble wobble toy. On her way forward, she stretched out her arms and shoved Murdy right back. She shoved her so hard that Murdy left the ground, flew backwards into the cart and crashed into the belly of the monster.

While Murdy scrambled about trying to get herself out, all the while shouting that Kay was for it, the cart started to creep ever so slowly down the hill. I went to grab it before it picked up more speed, but as I stepped towards it, I tripped up on the tennis-ball-eyeball that Mr Dog must have dropped near my feet. Then, before I knew what was happening, the mop bucket flew out of my hand and my feet were higher than my head.

I landed in the cart on top of Murdy and the monster parts, and the mop bucket landed on top of my head.

The impact of my fall created the extra momentum the cart needed, and we started rolling down the hill towards the loch, really, really fast.

I had no idea what was happening because my head was in a bucket and it was all echoey, because I was screaming very loudly asking all the gods and lords and goddesses to save us. Murdy told me later that we were quite lucky to plough into Uncle Hamish's Land Rover. He might not have seen it that way, but if we had been half a metre to the left, we would definitely have made it along the jetty and into the lake.

We may have been lucky, but our Loch Lochy Monster model was not. While gaffer tape is good for keeping hostages, it was not able to withstand the impact of hurtling into a Land Rover Defender at what felt like one thousand miles an hour. Our masterpiece ended up not only headless and eyeball-less, it also lost its tumble-dryer-tube tail, its body and its neck – all its monstery body parts, in fact. It was completely destroyed.

Uncle Hamish and Stanley came running out of the house when they heard the **CRASH**. They found me and Murdy sitting in a pile of Loch Lochy Monster pieces checking ourselves over for injuries, with Mr Dog next to us, tennis-ball-eyeball in his mouth, tail wagging.

Kay and the twins must have scarpered because they were nowhere to be seen. Even so, Murdy stood up and kicked the tumble-dryer hose and shouted, "You're lucky you legged it, McGavin! I've had enough, you hear me? I've had enough of you picking on me! I don't know why I ever cared when you just stopped being my friend!"

It is safe to say that our first monster attempt did not go magnificently. Sitting in among all the monster debris, I felt a tiny flicker of hopelessness. But I squashed that down smartish. I bet even Frankenstein didn't make his monster on his first go.

CHAPTER 19

A VERY BAD SIGN

The next morning, I didn't wake until quite late – monster building is an exhausting business. I found Uncle Hamish and Stanley outside; standing round the Land Rover surveying the massive dent in the driver's side door that the cart crash had created.

Uncle Hamish frowned when he saw me. "I'm very glad you weren't hurt, laddie, but remind me again, what *were* you and Murdy up to?"

I took a really deep breath. "Go-kart racing." Lying to Uncle Hamish wasn't easy. But I reminded myself of why I was doing it. I had to save the holiday lets. I had to show Stanley that impossible things could happen.

"I still don't understand why you needed the buoys."

"They were bumpers."

Stanley pointed at the dent. "Didn't work very well, did they?"

I shook my head. "No, Stanley, they did not."

Before either of them could question me any further, an expensive-looking car pulled up beside the house. We all knew who it was. Uncle Hamish ran his hand through his hair, and it stuck up on end, making him look even more stressed.

"What's that neep doing here?"

Gregor McGavin climbed out of the car, put on his sunglasses and inhaled really loudly, like he was trying to suck the whole place up his nose. Just as Uncle Hamish was saying, "Thought I told you to stay off my land," another guy got out of the car. He was about as wide as he was tall. He was also wearing a suit, but I reckon if he flexed his muscles, he'd rip right through it.

"Brought a friend to look after you?" Uncle Hamish said. "How nice."

"We've a little something for you," Gregor said and nodded at the other guy. Mr Muscles took his cue and walked up to Uncle Hamish and handed him an envelope.

"What's this, a present? You shouldn't have." Uncle Hamish was joking but nobody laughed.

"It's the end, Hamish," Gregor said.

Uncle Hamish stared at the envelope like it was an unexploded bomb. His face changed. He didn't look angry any more, he looked desperate. "You've got to give me more time, Gregor. I've had some big outgoings lately, but things will get better. I'll get you your money, I give you my word, but you can't take my home."

Gregor McGavin said, "You've already had more time. There's no more leeway. This property belongs to McGavin's bank now – that is unless you pay me double what you owe. You have one month to vacate the premises."

"Vacate the premises?" Uncle Hamish said, like he couldn't quite understand the words.

Stanley and I looked at each other.

"But this is my home. Our home. This place has been in my family for years. Gregor, please, we used to be friends."

Friends? I could not believe my lugholes. How could Uncle Hamish have been friends with a man like Gregor McGavin?

Gregor McGavin said, "This is business, don't make it personal. It's time to accept what's happening." Then he and the other guy walked past us, back to their car. Whilst Gregor got into the driver's seat, the muscly guy opened up the boot and pulled out a sign and a mallet. He hammered the sign into the ground, right outside the house, got back into the car and then they drove off.

The sign said, FORECLOSURE, LOCH LOCHY HOUSE AND HOLIDAY LETS in angry red letters.

"That's it then," Stanley said, with a sigh. "We'll be moving again."

"What's that mean –" I sounded out the word – "foreclosure?" It felt heavy in my mouth.

"It means McGavin is going to sell this place out from under us and use the money to pay back what Uncle Hamish owes."

Uncle Hamish looked at us both like he'd only just remembered we were there. "I'm sorry you had to see that. But don't worry, I'll figure something out." He tried to smile, but it made him seem even less convincing.

Stanley shrugged and said, "Whatever," like he wasn't bothered, but I couldn't believe that was true.

"Whatever happens," Uncle Hamish went on, "I want you boys to know that you'll be staying with me. I'll still look after you – you have my word on that."

It was nice of Uncle Hamish to say that, but really it was pretty obvious that it was him who was the one who needed looking after. He was about to lose everything and, as far as I could tell, he didn't know what to do about it. Loch Lochy was his anchor, and since we'd arrived, it was the first time following Mum and Dad's disappearance that I hadn't felt completely adrift.

We all stood there, not speaking – the foreclosure sign taunting us. It looked so official, so final. At that moment, Gregor McGavin and his bank seemed more powerful and more terrifying than any loch monster.

The enormity of the situation began to sink in, and I started to worry that there was nothing we could do –

that my whole plan to defraud people with photos of a pretend loch monster was ridiculous. How could it possibly work? Gregor McGavin practically owned the whole town; a kid – even a visionary one like me – wasn't going to be able to stop him getting what he wanted. But then Mr Dog trotted up to the sign, cocked his leg and did a truly massive Niagara Falls-style pee on the stake.

"Well at least we know what Mr Dog thinks of that," Stanley said.

I think Mr Dog's huge urination must have stirred up something defiant in Uncle Hamish because he said, "You know what? Mr Dog is right." He stomped over to the sign, wrapped his massive hands round the stake and pulled it straight out of the ground with only two heaves! Then he ran to the edge of the lake, his great long legs taking giant strides, and with an almighty roar, like a proper Scottish clansman, hurled the sign into the water.

"That is what I think of your sign, Gregor McGavin, you wee, greasy-haired goon!"

It was very exhilarating to watch. I cheered, Mr Dog

barked and jumped up and down and Stanley stood there, taking it all in before saying, "You probably want to fetch that back out – you can't go chucking rubbish into the water," which totally ruined the mutinous mood, but Uncle Hamish said he did have a point.

While Uncle Hamish tried to pull the sign back out of the water without falling in, I made a promise to myself. I wasn't going to let one failed attempt stop me. I had less than three weeks to create my monster evidence. Less than three weeks to save Loch Lochy. Less than three weeks to show Stanley I was right to believe in the impossible.

I was going to create the Monster of Loch Lochy and nothing would stop me.

CHAPTER 20

A REBUILD?

Murdy turned up not long after Uncle Hamish had retrieved the foreclosure sign from the loch. Her mum had driven her to ours because she wanted to speak to Uncle Hamish. When she saw him carrying the sign, Clara said, "Oh, Hamish, it's got this far?"

Uncle Hamish forced a smile and put the sign upside down in the wheelie bin. "It's not the end yet, Clara. I'll figure something out."

Stanley whispered to me, "He keeps saying that, but I don't see him doing much figuring."

Murdy looked at me with big dramatic eyes and said, "It's all been going on here, hasn't it?"

Clara slammed the car door shut. "Let's get inside

and talk, shall we?" She held a battered Quality Street tin in one hand and a string bag in the other. "I brought cake and oranges."

I was keen to get on and start a new, more visionary Loch Lochy Monster model involving less gaffer tape, but cake was quite a pull and who doesn't like an orange? Also, I'm pretty sure brains are at their most visionary and creative once they've had proper nutrition, so I decided to stick around for a snack and listen to what the grown-ups had to say.

We all sat round the kitchen table, us kids keeping quiet while Uncle Hamish and Clara talked about ways they could solve Uncle Hamish's financial situation. Mr Dog's face appeared between my legs, and I gave him a wodge of my Victoria Sponge and pretended not to ear waggle their conversation as they whispered to each other at the other end of the table.

"There's no way you can cut your outgoings?" Clara said. "The money you're spending on—"

Uncle Hamish shook his head and gave her a weird look. Clara glanced from me to Stanley and stopped talking.

"That can't happen. It is a necessity," he continued. "There must be another way."

Stanley said, "What's a necessity?"

But Uncle Hamish didn't really answer. Instead he gave Clara a look and said, "Oh, nothing important."

Stanley gave Uncle Hamish a look of his own and muttered, "It's always important."

I didn't think any more of it at the time. I just figured necessities meant boring things like paying for electricity and heating. But it turns out necessities mean different things to different people.

I considered telling Uncle Hamish about the loch-monster plan, but when I said, "Uncle Hamish, I might have an idea," he said, "This is adult talk now, Benji. I appreciate your support but it's best you leave this to us."

Stanley stood up, clearly annoyed, and said, "I'm going to read my book." Then off he stomped, swiping an orange from the table.

I decided it was probably best I didn't tell Uncle Hamish what I was up to but, frankly, the ideas he and Clara mentioned over tea were not very visionary *at all*.

They basically involved going to other banks and begging to borrow money from them to pay off Gregor. That seemed a bit strange to me – if he borrowed money he'd still end up owing money. It wasn't solving the problem, just putting the problem somewhere else. But to be honest, Uncle Hamish didn't give me the impression that he was going to be open to discussing more creative ways to raise cash, so I didn't push it.

I raised my eyebrows at Murdy. "Shall we go?"

"Aye." She rammed the last of her cake in her mouth, spraying crumbs about, which Mr Dog quickly hoovered up.

Uncle Hamish eyed us suspiciously. "I hope you two aren't up to any more go-kart adventures."

"We are absolutely not going to be doing that," I said, very honestly.

"Hmm. Keep an eye on them, Mr Dog."

Mr Dog looked from me to Murdy then gave a little whine, like Uncle Hamish was asking a bit too much of him.

Clara gave Murdy a stern look. "Stay out of mischief, Murdy Mei-Yin McGurdy."

Murdy gave her a decidedly mischievous grin in return.

As we made our way to the garage, I summed up the situation. "Look," I said, "we did not get the outcome we wanted yesterday, but, while our execution was not the best, I don't think our idea is a bad one."

"I agree," Murdy said. "We just need to build a better monster."

"Exactly." I was pleased Murdy and I were thinking along the same lines. I pulled open the garage doors and switched on the light. Mr Dog found himself a nice spot and curled up between two bags of fertilizer.

I plopped myself down on the workbench and Murdy wrestled an old-looking deckchair open and then sat down on that.

"How do you think we should do it – build a better monster?" I asked.

"No idea. Glue?"

I scrunched up my nose. "What like Pritt Stick?"

"No, you eejit, like superglue. There's that stuff POWER PASTE. Mum's got loads of it. Dad used to fix things properly, but since he left Mum just slaps that on anything that's broken. It's really strong. In the advert they stick a man to a wall with it."

"That's exactly what we need."

"Why do you need to stick a man to a wall?" Stanley was standing in the garage door with his hands on his hips, managing to look angry and mistrusting at the same time.

"Stanley, what are you doing here?" I said, trying to sound casual, but not really succeeding.

He narrowed his eyes and repeated the question. "Benji, why do you want to stick a man to a wall?"

I shot Murdy a desperate glance, hoping she might come to my rescue, but she just shrugged. I suppose I can't blame her. It's not like there's an obvious explanation when you're caught talking about gluing someone to a building.

I decided I may as well be honest and tell him. I had wanted to show him evidence of the real Loch Lochy Monster to get him to believe in the impossible. But right then, maybe I just needed him to believe in me, because in that moment the most impossible task seemed to be stopping Gregor McGavin. Maybe after the whole sign thing, Stanley might realize how desperate the situation was and offer to help.

"We don't want to stick a man to a wall. We want to build a Loch Lochy Monster."

Stanley took a moment before saying, very slowly, "You want to build a Loch Lochy Monster?"

"Uh-huh. Want to help?"

He didn't answer for several seconds again, then said even more slowly, "Why do you want to build a Loch Lochy Monster?"

Murdy said, "Because the first one fell apart when we ploughed into the side of the Land Rover."

Stanley stared at me. "What?"

"It's true. I blame the gaffer tape."

Stanley said, "*What?*" again.

"We're building a Loch Lochy Monster because we can't find the real one," Murdy said.

"And until it shows up again, we have to have some way of getting tourists to Loch Lochy so Uncle Hamish can rake in loads of cash and tell Gregor McGavin to do one." I realized I was speaking really fast, but I couldn't help it, I just wanted to tell him everything. "It might sound like fraud, but it isn't really because the Loch Lochy Monster does actually exist, Stanley! You have to believe me – it just isn't keen on having its photo taken. Which is very inconvenient, so we're sort of working around that." I stopped and stared at him, desperate for him to respond.

After a few moments, Stanley shook his head and looked at me like I'd grown extra elbows. "That *thing* that crashed into the Land Rover was supposed to be a loch monster?"

"You didn't see it at its best," I told him. "So, do you want to help? We could use your expertise. You're dead good at building things. Go on, say you will."

He looked like he was actually considering it, but I must have read him wrong, because he laughed and said, "I've got better things to do than waste my time building a loch monster for some ridiculous plan from the bizarre brain of Benji McLaughlin."

I would have asked him what better things, but he'd walked off.

"Looks like it's just us then," Murdy said.

I said, "Probably better this way to be honest," but I

didn't really believe that. Before, Stanley had always been happy to get involved in my plans. I might be visionary, but Stanley was the person who could make my visions a reality. Like the time I built a den in our garden, and he solved my roofing problem by using Dad's surfboard. Or when I decided I'd see if I could get my bike to fly by adding wings. He was the one who helped me build the ramp and bolt the plastic and coat-hanger glider onto the frame. He also suggested I wear a helmet and elbow and knee protectors. We'd always been a team.

Deep down, I always knew I needed Stanley.

CHAPTER 21

ALONE ON THE JETTY

aving decided that the failure of the first monster model was largely down to the gaffer tape, Murdy and I both felt that we should approach the build of Loch Lochy Monster version 2.0 in a similar manner – selecting monstery-looking body parts from our garage and shed supplies and joining them together – but this time with the brilliant bonding capabilities of Power Paste. Believe me, that stuff is strong! And we had loads of it. Murdy's mum had a whole cupboard full of the stuff. There must have been a lot of broken things in the McGurdy household.

You have to be extremely careful using Power Paste.

I learned that the hard way, when I accidentally glued the mop-bucket monster head to the workbench and the Power Paste tube to the mop bucket. When I tried to pull it all apart, I put my foot against the workbench to give me some leverage and glued my trainer to it too. Mr Dog got one of the tennis-ball-eyeballs stuck to his tail fur and ended up running round in circles trying to chase it. I think he was having fun to start with, but eventually he figured out it was a game he was never going to win and got a bit frustrated and started barking. I couldn't help because I was still stuck to the workbench dealing with my own glue-related foot problem. I suppose it was all quite chaotic.

Murdy let out a big, exasperated scream and threw her arms in the air. "I can't work like this!"

I stopped tugging at my foot and Mr Dog stopped running in circles and Murdy gave us a bit of a telling-off and made us promise to be more careful.

Murdy set my foot free, cut the tennis ball off Mr Dog's tail and then we continued rebuilding the monster with Murdy in sole charge of the Power Paste. By the time we had put the monster parts back together, I think both Murdy and I had come to the realization that our model was not as convincing as we had originally thought. We stood back to assess our handiwork.

"What do you think?" I asked.

Murdy's nose crinkled. "Do you want the truth?"

"Always."

"I'm not as positive as I was yesterday."

I flopped down on the deckchair. "Nor am I. Frankly, Kay McGavin was right. It looks like some sort of weird camel."

"Who's to say that tourists won't flock in to see a camel-ish loch monster?" Murdy said.

We both looked at the model again, tilting our heads and hoping a different angle would somehow improve what we'd created.

"Would you pay to come and see that?" I asked.

She ummed for a bit then said, "No, probably not. It doesn't exactly scream BIG SCARY LOCH MONSTER, does it?"

"No, it does not. I hate to admit it, but we're going to have to come up with another idea." I got to my feet. "But I don't think we're going to find inspiration sitting in here looking at that heap of junk. Let's go for a walk by the loch."

Murdy, Mr Dog and I walked down the hill to the path that hugged the loch. I took her to the place where I'd first seen the Loch Lochy Monster and we both shimmied up Dad's tree and sat on the branch. I didn't point out the carvings to her. I wanted to show them to Stanley before anyone else. That only seemed right.

"Nice how the sun makes the water all spinkly-sparkly," I said.

I thought she was going to take the mickey out me for being so poetic, but she didn't, she just said, "Aye – hard to believe there's a monster in there somewhere."

"Some things *are* hard to believe – it doesn't mean they're not true."

"Aye," Murdy said before shouting, "Where are you, Loch Lochy Monster? We know you're there somewhere!"

I think we were both hoping that the monster would appear. We fell silent, our eyes scanning the water for a ripple or a splash. Willing it to show itself.

But we didn't see a monster. We saw Stanley.

"Is that your brother?" Murdy asked, shielding
her eyes.

I nodded. We were quite far away but I could tell by
the way he was standing, with his shoulders hunched
over, that it was him. He was on the jetty wearing his
swimmers and carrying a towel under his arm.

"Looks like he's going for a swim," Murdy said casually.

A swim? That couldn't be right – not with the way he felt about the water. I leaned forward, trying to get a better look. Slowly, Stanley walked to the end of the pier and put his towel on the ground. Then he looked out across the loch. I thought he might see us, but his mind must have been on other, bigger things. I felt my heart beating hard in my chest for him.

Get in the water, Stanley. Go on, you can do it.

He waited at the top of the ladder for quite some time, as though he was trying to pluck up the courage. Then he lowered a foot onto the first rung, and I held my breath.

You can do it, Stanley.

Then he climbed down to the second rung and then the third.

Almost there, Stan.

He reached the rung of the ladder which was just above the surface of the water, and he stopped. He stayed there, frozen for ages, and I had to quit holding my breath or I would have passed out from lack of oxygen.

Go on, Stanley, get in.

"What's he doing?" Murdy asked, but I shushed her.

He was trying. That's what he was doing. And it was both incredible and painful to witness.

My heart dipped when Stanley began to climb back up the ladder. He picked up his towel and walked back down the jetty.

"Your brother's weird," Murdy said.

"He's not weird," I snapped. "He's scared of the water."

Murdy screwed up her face. "Why? Because of the Loch Lochy Monster?"

"No, because of what he saw."

"What do you mean *what he saw*?"

I took a breath and the words rushed out. "He was there when the boat my parents were on capsized. He was found clinging to the hull six hours after it happened. He was out in the water, all alone."

As I watched his retreating figure, it struck me how utterly alone he must still feel. It was as though part of him was still clinging on to that boat. Clinging on to what had happened. Clinging on so hard, he wasn't able to let go and reach out.

Murdy shook her head. "That must have been awful."

"He's not been able to get in a boat or swim since. Although he won't admit it."

"Understandable," Murdy said. "He won't talk about it then?"

"No, not to me, anyway."

Stanley had never been able to speak to me about that day. Everything I knew, which wasn't much, had come from counsellors.

Murdy nodded, then, very gently, said, "And where were you, Benji, when it happened? You don't have to tell me if you don't want to."

I looked at my lap, not wanting to meet Murdy's gaze. "I was at a kids' club. Painting pebbles."

It sounded so stupid. Guilt swirled in my stomach. It might not be easy to understand, but I wish I'd been there too. I was part of the family; I should have been there with them.

"You were lucky," she said, which was both right and wrong. Then she hesitated, "Did Stanley...you know...see your parents dr—"

"They didn't drown, Murdy," I said, angrily. "They're still alive."

"But if they haven't been seen in—"

"No *but if*s. I know they are still alive."

"How do you know they're still alive, Benji?" Murdy said softly.

"I know they're still alive because I still feel them." I put my fist on my chest. "I feel them right here. I know it's hard to believe, but it doesn't mean it's not true."

Murdy put her hand on mine and looked out at the loch. "I believe you."

And Mr Dog, who was sitting on the ground below us did this small whimpering noise which very much sounded like, "I believe you too."

I turned my head away from Murdy. I wanted to check my dad's name was still there, etched into his tree. I blinked away the tears which had found their way out of my eyes and looked back over towards Stanley. I wished, more than anything, I could go over to him and give him a hug. I wished with my entire everything that the distance between us wasn't so big.

CHAPTER 22

YOU CAN'T GO WRONG
WITH CAKE

Inspiration about how to build a new and improved loch monster model did not strike me or Murdy that afternoon. I was on a bit of a downer after accidentally crying halfway up Dad's tree, so I wasn't at my most visionary.

And I really wasn't in the mood for it when, on our way home, we ran into Kay McGavin and Camilla and Clarissa. Murdy grabbed my hand and tried to pull me behind a bush, but Mr Dog blew our cover by running up to them and barking in his friendly manner, his tail wagging joyfully. I wouldn't change Mr Dog for the world, but in that moment I wished he wasn't quite so clueless.

"We see you, Murdy McGurdy!" Kay hollered as she started down the path towards us.

"Here we go," I muttered.

"Yeah, we see you, Murdy McGurdy," Camilla and Clarissa repeated, in freakishly exact unison.

"Well now we've established your eyeballs are working," Murdy said, springing out from the undergrowth, "is there anything else we can help you with?"

Kay jabbed her finger at Murdy. "Don't get smart with me, Little Miss Liar-Pants."

Before I could say something to prevent us from getting into a fight, Murdy rolled back her shoulders and said, "Why, are you too stupid to follow?"

The twins' mouths dropped open like those carp fish things you see in garden centre ponds. Kay's cheeks turned so scarlet she looked like a boiled lobster, and I started to wonder if Murdy might have a death wish.

"Are you calling me stupid?" Kay asked, taking a giant step towards us with her massive feet.

I gulped. "She's not calling you stupid."

"I am," Murdy said, unhelpfully.

"Look, we don't want any trouble," I continued, "we just want to get home."

Kay raised an eyebrow. "I should be quick, if I were you. Something tells me that's not going to be your home for much longer."

I stepped round her and very quietly, so I didn't feel like I was completely losing face, said, "We'll see about that."

Murdy followed behind and said much more loudly, "Yeah, we'll see about that."

Kay laughed and shouted after us, "Dad says he's going to bulldoze this place to the ground. Get the diggers in and rip out the rot and build some smart, modern-looking buildings. Put some hot tubs on the balconies. Proper luxury."

"Proper luxury," Clarissa and Camilla repeated.

I didn't react and kept on walking. I have to admit that while hot tubs did not sound like a *terrible* idea, I did not like the thought of bulldozers flattening our home. Or diggers ripping out Dad's tree from the roots. I felt a bubble of panic blooming in my chest. *Our home.* I had thought of it as *our* home. Even though I hadn't been there that long, I realized in that exact moment, that I did feel like part of me belonged to Loch Lochy and I belonged to it. Maybe there was some of the loch running through my veins too. Maybe the part of me that was Dad.

Murdy and I were going to have to come up with a new idea to get our monster evidence and fast.

It was when I was filling Mr Dog's bowl with Pedigree Chum later that evening that inspiration finally struck.

Mr Dog charged onto the porch the moment I set his dinner down. "That's it!" I shouted. Mr Dog didn't look up from his food, but I told him my new visionary idea anyway. "Tomorrow, Mr Dog, we're going Loch Lochy Monster fishing."

That did get his attention. He looked up at me with puzzled eyes.

"Don't you see, Mr Dog?" I said, excitedly pacing up and down the decking. "What we need to do is lure the monster with some sort of bait. What do you think?"

Mr Dog's eyes grew as big as his food bowl, and he let out a little whimper.

I bent down and gave him a hug. "I didn't mean you, Mr Dog, you dafty! You're my best friend, I'd never use you for monster bait! I promise I'd never let anything bad happen to you."

Before I could tell him it wasn't necessary, Mr Dog gave me a big lick across my face. I appreciated the sentiment, but it was pretty gross. His tongue smelled of his poultry-flavoured dog food.

That evening I laid in bed trying to think of a way to speak to Stanley about his aborted swimming attempt, but I couldn't think of the right words. It didn't seem like he wanted to talk, because when I said, "Stanleyyyyy?" he just said, "Reading," and stuck his face further into his book. So I looked up at the ceiling and let myself get a bit excited about how successful my monster-fishing expedition was going to be and how happy Uncle Hamish would be when I told him that I'd found a way to get the holidaymakers back.

Just as I was imagining Uncle Hamish lifting me up and swinging me around like Dad used to do, Uncle

Hamish popped his head through the door and said, "Knock, knock?"

"Who's there?" I said, because I thought it would be funny, but I don't think Uncle Hamish got my joke, because he said in a confused-sounding voice, "It's me...your uncle Hamish."

He came into the room and stood in the middle of the rug, shifting his weight from foot to foot and generally looking a bit awkward.

"Soooooo," he said swinging his arms then rubbing his hands together.

"Soooooo?" I said.

Stanley closed his book. "Did you want something?"

Uncle Hamish motioned towards Stanley's bed, I think to ask to sit down on it. Stanley gave a shrug which Uncle Hamish took to be permission and he plonked himself down so heavily, I'm surprised he didn't catapult Stanley out of it. Then he rubbed his hands together and said, "Sooooo," again.

"Is there something we can help you with, Uncle Hamish?" I asked brightly because he looked like he needed some positive encouragement.

"I just thought I'd come in, and say hi, you know...
so...hi."

"Hi, Uncle Hamish," I said. "Say hi, Stanley."

Stanley actually said, "Hi," rather than just grunting,
which felt like progress so I gave him a thumbs up, but
he just pulled a face at me and told me to stop being
weird.

"I guess I just wanted to check in with you two. See
how you're doing after that little run-in with that wee
neep Gregor and all this foreclosure business."

"We're fine," I said. "How are you doing?"

"Me? Och, you know, how could I be anything other
than dazzling having you two here? I also came to let
you know, Stanley, that Sandra, the lady from social
services up here, has organized for you to speak to a
counsellor tomorrow. She'll ring first. Take it from
there type thing."

Stanley nodded and said, "Thanks," then looked at
me. "What about Benji?"

"What about me?" I said.

"Do you want to speak to someone?" Uncle Hamish
said. "I can definitely arrange that."

"No, thank you very much," I said. "I already graduated from counselling."

Uncle Hamish stood up and gave me a wink. "Alright then, kiddos. Lights out in ten, okay?"

We listened to Uncle Hamish's big galumphing footsteps and when we heard the living room door close, Stanley said, "You should think about speaking to a counsellor again."

"Nah," I said and turned out the light. I didn't need counselling. I had a Loch Lochy Monster plan and a head full of hope.

The following morning, I arranged to meet Murdy outside the village shop. She'd been very positive about my new monster-fishing plan.

"It's a shame we didn't come up with it before we spent hours building a model. I'm surprised we didn't think of it before," she said as I was tying Mr Dog to a post outside.

She was right but there was nothing we could do about that now.

"Did you get it?" I asked.

Murdy pointed at her T-shirt – well my T-shirt – and

said, "Aye, course I did, because I am awesome!"

"I'm not ever getting that T-shirt back, am I?"

She didn't answer, just grinned and pulled her da's old camera out of the back pocket of her shorts. "I put new batteries in. Wouldn't want them running out when the monster appears now, would we?"

"Nice work. You know I've got a good feeling about this plan." I grabbed a basket from by the swooshy doors and said, "What food do you think a loch monster would like the most?"

"Not a clue," Murdy said as we started down the fruit and veg aisle.

"There's a good offer on cauliflowers," I told her.

"I don't think a couple of caulies are going to tempt the monster from the deep," she said, probably accurately.

"Do you think the loch monster is a vegetarian though?" I asked.

"Impossible to say," she said. "More likely one of those pescatarians Mum says everyone seems to be turning into, so perhaps we should avoid meat-based products just in case."

She was probably right about that too, so I put the bumper pack of Peperami I was holding back on the shelf.

We carried on wandering through the aisles, hoping inspiration would strike again.

"What would I want to eat if I were a loch monster?" I said out loud. "Probably not fish – I imagine that it has fish all the time. What we need is a treat."

"A treat for a loch monster," Murdy said, mulling it over.

I chose to ignore how ridiculous that sounded.

"Can't go wrong with cake," Murdy said, pausing by the baked goods.

"That's true. Everyone likes cake. I can't see why a loch monster would be any different."

So that was decided and, armed with several boxes of Mrs McPopling's finest bakes and a lot of positive thoughts, we headed back to where the rowing boat was moored beside the loch.

CHAPTER 23

A CHANGE OF HEART

I have to admit, I was feeling ever so positive about my plan to get a photo of the Loch Lochy Monster by tempting him into sight with a few fondant fancies. It made me completely forget about any fear I might have about actually coming face to face with the monster again. "You see, Murdy," I said as I pushed the boat out into the water, "the plan's genius is in its simplicity."

"Oh aye, is that so?" Murdy said as she began paddling in time with me.

"What we must do, is make sure we move ourselves to a safe distance once the cake-bait is in the water. We don't want to fall overboard like last time so no dangling over the edge, understand?"

She stopped rowing and glared at me. "You were the one who let go of my legs."

For team morale, I decided it was best not to get into it, so I said very brightly, "I think this looks like an excellent spot. Shall we put out the bait?"

Mr Dog padded over from his usual spot at the front of the boat and looked at me expectantly.

"I'm sorry, Mr Dog, all the cakes are for the monster."

He tilted his head and gave a little whine.

"Och, one each wouldn't hurt, would it?" Murdy said.

I looked in the shopping bags. "I suppose we do have loads."

"And we wouldn't want to give the Loch Lochy Monster an acute case of diabetes now, would we?" Murdy said.

"This is very true."

"Just one or two each," Murdy continued, "and the monster can have the rest."

So, sitting under the mid-morning sun, at a safe distance from where we had thrown the remaining cake-bait, we ate three cakes each and scanned the water, hoping the Loch Lochy Monster had a hankering for a cherry bakewell or lemon drizzle slice.

After forty minutes, my optimism began to fade. Several little fish were nibbling away at the bits of cake that were dispersing across the loch, but there was no sign of the monster.

"Maybe those Peperami might have been more tempting after all," Murdy said.

"I don't think you can get any more tempting than Mrs McPopling's finest," I replied, feeling very deflated. Loch monster fishing had felt quite exciting when I thought I might actually catch the Loch Lochy Monster – well, with a camera at any rate. Now I just felt like a bit of an idiot, sitting in a boat which was surrounded by soggy Battenberg.

I think something – maybe desperation – must have come over me because before I knew what I was doing, I was standing up in the boat shouting out across the water. "Where are you, Loch Lochy Monster? All we want is one photo. Is that too much to ask? I'm begging you, pleading with you to show yourself. We need you, Loch Lochy Monster! Please give me a sign that you're there. A flipper or a fin, or something!!"

I think because I was doing a lot of quite noisy begging and pleading, I was not aware of the McGavins' speedboat hurtling across the loch not too far away from us.

I did become aware of it very quickly, when the waves from their boat rocked ours so violently that I fell overboard, face first into a load of soggy sponge.

"Benji! What are you doing?" Murdy shouted at me.

"What does it look like I'm doing?" I shouted back as I flapped about in the water, very glad the loch monster hadn't decided to pay us a visit.

"It looks like you've decided to go for a swim during

our loch monster search."

Murdy helped drag me back onto the boat by the shoulders of my life jacket. Well, she pulled me halfway on, so I was hanging over the side, and then she sort of threw her hands away in disgust.

"Not again! I'm blinded!" she shouted, covering her face. "I told you to keep that peely-wally backside of yours covered."

I scrambled aboard and quickly pulled my shorts up. "I'll get a belt," I told her as Mr Dog licked the cake gloop off my legs.

"I think perhaps that's a sign it's time to call it a day and head back to shore," Murdy said, carefully opening her eyes.

I had to agree. The Loch Lochy Monster clearly wasn't going to surface and the sight of Gregor McGavin motoring about on the loch was too much.

As we moored the boat by the pier, and took off our life jackets, I said to Murdy, "I think we're going to have to come up with *another* solution."

"Whatever it is," she said, "could it not involve you waggling your bare bum about?"

"Well, *obviously*. Don't worry, I'll think of something."
I tried to sound positive but, to be honest, I was beginning to think I might have run out of ideas. I had a horrible feeling that Gregor McGavin actually stood a chance of taking our home.

Luckily, something strange and unexpected happened that very evening.

Stanley came to the rescue.

Clara had just collected Murdy, and Stanley and I were up in our room. I had my eyes shut trying to be visionary but failing and Stanley was reading again. He went off to the loo and was gone for so long I began to wonder if he might have fallen in. When he finally got back, he had this really odd look on his face. He sat on his bed, his hands steepled under his chin like he was thinking very hard about something. I wondered if maybe he wanted to speak about his failed swimming attempt the day before – perhaps it had been playing on his mind and he was finally ready to talk.

"Is everything okay?"

He didn't hear me, so I said it again.

"Earth to Stanley – everything okay? I saw you on the pier yesterday."

"What?"

"Stan, you look a bit weird. Has something happened? Do you want to talk about it? Your water thing maybe?"

He said, "It's not about the water," and then he said something more unexpected than a visit from an alien spaceship from the Tri-galaxy. "I want to help you build your monster."

I think I shouted, "What?"

"You heard. I want to help you build your monster."

"You do? Why?" It was all very surprising. He'd been so against the idea before.

He shrugged. "No reason."

"But I thought you didn't believe there was a monster."

"I don't, but I think your idea might just work. If you do it properly."

I did not know what happened in the loo to change his mind – I found out much later – but I decided that it didn't really matter. I was just thrilled he was going

239

to help. With Stanley on board with his intelligence and excellent building skills, we might stand a chance of making a monster model before it was too late. Besides, I was worried if I pushed him for an explanation he might change his mind, so I said, "Stanley, that's great news, thank you."

He opened the top drawer of his bedside table and pulled out a notepad. "I'll come up with a design. We can set about building it tomorrow." He didn't look at me, just began scribbling away like it was no big deal.

"I...I...I don't know what to say, Stanley."

"You have to agree to do what I tell you, or I'm not helping." He picked up his engineering book and flicked through until he found the page he wanted. "I'm in charge of the build."

I wasn't sure how I felt about relinquishing my control, but as the gaffer taping and Power Pasting hadn't gone fabulously and I had no new idea of my own, I knew I had to swallow my pride. "Sure, Stanley, I'll do as you say."

And I did. Murdy, however, was a bit more reluctant about following orders.

CHAPTER 24

A NEW MAGNIFICENT MONSTER

I thought the plans Stanley showed Murdy, Mr Dog and me for his monster were great – way better than anything we had come up with but, for some reason, Murdy didn't seem that impressed.

We were sitting on the jetty, with Stanley's plans spread out on the floor in front of us. Murdy spent a while looking at them, making various tutting sounds. Then she sat back on her knees, screwed up her face and said, "That looks way too complicated. There's no way we're going to be able to make that."

Stanley wasn't worried though. He chucked a pebble in the loch, then said, very confidently, "There's every way we're going to make it. I know what I'm doing. You're working with a pro now."

Murdy didn't look sure. She screwed up her face even tighter and gestured at the monster plan. "How are you going to attach all the bits? Before you say it, we've tried tape and glue and neither of those worked."

"Shocker," Stanley said. "We'll use a drill, of course. And nuts and bolts."

"What's that part?" I asked, pointing at a large rectangular shape on his plan.

"It's a tin bathtub. There's one round the back of one of the holiday houses – Bonnie, I think."

"And this bit?"

Stanley pulled a face. "That's the neck."

"It looks familiar – what's it made of?"

"That, Benji, is the snorkel off the Land Rover."

"Stanley! We cannot steal the snorkel off the Land Rover! It's Uncle Hamish's pride and joy!"

"Can you think of anything more neck shaped? We'll put it back afterwards," he said incorrectly. "What do you think of the flippers? They will actually paddle – see, I've drawn a motorized pedal system inside."

He flipped the plans round and showed us a detailed drawing of a load of cogs and two sets of bike pedals that were attached to some feet. It was the most visionary plan I had ever seen.

"Stanley!" I gasped. "Do you mean it will actually swim – like a real loch monster?"

"It will swim, but not like a real loch monster – what with them not existing and all."

To be honest, I was too busy marvelling at Stanley's fantastic plan to call him out on his startling lack of belief. And, when I looked at his eyes, I saw something in them that I hadn't seen in a long time. A light. A glimmer of the Stanley from before.

"It is excellent, Stanley. Truly," I said, my voice wobbling from the sudden emotion I was feeling. "Don't you think so, Murdy?"

Murdy's face unscrunched a little and she waved her hand at the plan. "You actually think we can build that?"

"Aye, wee lassie," Stanley said, the smallest of smiles flickering on his lips. "I do."

Murdy nodded decisively. "Well, we best get going then."

Stanley, unsurprisingly, was a very stern taskmaster. He sent Murdy and me out to collect everything we needed while he prepared his tools and did other important stuff. What that important stuff was, I don't know, because when we got back with our last load of monster parts, he was sat in the deckchair eating a Penguin – you know which type – and reading a magazine. He didn't get up while he instructed us what order to lay out the bits on the garage floor. He was very specific – apparently it is very important to be organized when building a Loch Lochy Monster. The only thing Murdy, Mr Dog and I hadn't collected was the snorkel from the Land Rover and that was because Uncle Hamish was in town talking to some new bank manager. Probably about another loan. We were laying out the last part when we heard the growl of the engine and then his footsteps heading towards the garage.

He poked his head in and said, "What's going on in here? This all looks very interesting."

I must have panicked because I shouted, "We are doing nothing at all in here that is of any interest to you whatsoever. We are being completely and utterly uninteresting. So completely uninteresting—"

Murdy elbowed me, which was a good thing because it made me stop rambling.

Uncle Hamish's eyebrows lowered like they didn't believe me. "You look very guilty, Benji."

I tried my best to force my face into an innocent expression. "I am very not guilty of anything, Uncle Hamish. I am very innocent, and I am being very uninteresting."

"You're being something alright," Murdy whispered, "totally weird."

Uncle Hamish looked over to Stanley. "What's going on in here?"

Stanley got up from the deckchair and, keeping his

cool, said, "Just, you know, tinkering about. We thought we might see what we could make out of some scrap."

Uncle Hamish still looked a bit suspicious, but before he could say anything Stanley continued. "How did it go today, Uncle Hamish? This must be a very stressful time for you. I want you to know I am very grateful for everything you are doing. Very grateful. Truly."

It was the first nice thing Stanley had said to Uncle Hamish since we'd arrived at Loch Lochy. It must have taken Uncle Hamish by surprise, because he sort of spluttered his reply.

"That's nice, very nice, of you...well, I don't know what to say. Thank you, Stanley, thank you. But don't you worry, everything is fine."

Thinking about it now, I should have realized that there was something about Stanley's voice that sounded sincere, but at the time I thought he was just trying to stop Uncle Hamish from getting suspicious. I didn't know about the real reason for his change of attitude until later.

After Uncle Hamish had left, Stanley picked up a

screwdriver and said, "Right, let's go get ourselves a monster neck."

I still wasn't one hundred per cent comfortable about pulling bits off Uncle Hamish's pride and joy, but Stanley said we needed the snorkel and, for some reason, I trusted him about that.

We didn't do a completely dreadful job of the extraction. Stanley used a penknife he'd found in the garage. Only a little bit of paint came off the bodywork, but that was barely noticeable next to the massive dent from the crash. I must have looked a little regretful, because after Murdy and I had loaded the snorkel into the cart, Stanley put his hand on my shoulder and said, "Don't worry, it's for a good cause. It's for Uncle Hamish."

I looked at him, wide-eyed. "You are being very nice about Uncle Hamish, Stanley."

He shrugged. "I guess he's kind of alright, you know?"

"Yes, I do know! I think he's very alright! And you are very alright too, Stanley! The best!"

Stanley rolled his eyes, but I could see he was trying

to stop himself from smiling. "Let's get going, shall we?"

"This will work, won't it?" I asked, suddenly full of doubt and worry. "We're running out of time."

Stanley said, "We'll have to wait and see. I imagine there's enough people daft enough to believe a Loch Lochy Monster exists, if we show them plausible evidence. And my design is as good as it's going to get. I've thought of everything."

Stanley's confidence made me feel confident. But he hadn't thought of everything. He hadn't thought about the plug.

CHAPTER 25

LAUNCHING THE
LOCH LOCHY MONSTER

It took us several days of hard work for us to build Stanley's visionary model. Murdy and I spent our time following orders – fetching things, finding the correct tools and holding things in place – while Stanley did all the proper work, but that was okay because we could see that he knew what he was doing. Our Loch Lochy Monster began to take shape. It started to look convincing. And by the time we had finished, it had working paddly feet, an excellent neck and a very mighty tail. It looked dark and menacing. It was very Loch Lochy Monstery.

The very same evening we finished our creation,

Stanley and I watched from the top of the stairs until Uncle Hamish had fallen asleep in front of the television. Then, with Mr Dog at our heels, we tiptoed out of the house to the garage to get our monster. Stanley pulled off the tarpaulin that we had hidden it under in a very dramatic fashion and said in a very terrifying voice, "I have created a monster and it will DESTROY you!"

Because I was feeling a bit anxious, I didn't realize he was joking and my voice went a bit squeaky when I said, "What? Why would you do that? That wasn't the plan!"

He chuckled. "Seriously, Benji? It's kind of a line from *Frankenstein* the movie."

I said, "I knew that," even though I did not.

We had agreed to meet Murdy at dusk to take the video evidence that would convince the world that there was a monster in our loch. Meeting at dusk had been my excellent idea because, from what I had heard, dusk is a time when exciting things happen. When Murdy and Stanley had asked me what time dusk was exactly, I wasn't one hundred per cent certain, but I said 9.30 p.m. because that sounded possible.

With a bit of effort, Stanley and I loaded the Loch Lochy Monster up onto the cart and we were off down the hill towards the loch. When we got to the waterside, Murdy was already waiting for us. She was dressed head to toe in black. Full balaclava and everything.

"You about to hold up a bank or something?" Stanley asked.

She pulled up her balaclava. She'd obviously created a lot of heat on her cycle over, because her head was steaming in the cold summer night. She rolled her eyes at Stanley. "No, I'm being incognito. But if this doesn't work, maybe I *will* hold up a bank –" then she looked at me and said – "again." Which I think was a joke. Probably.

Stanley rolled up his sleeves, which was the signal that he was about to get bossy. "It is going to work, and this is what we're going to do. We'll push the monster into the water from the end of the jetty. You two will go out in the boat, attach the model to the back with a tow rope, then you'll paddle it out into the middle of the loch, turn on the paddles and row out of shot. I'll stay on the jetty and film it all on my phone from there."

"Are you sure you don't want to launch your monster?" Murdy asked. "It was all your brainwork after all. You should get to go out in the boat."

Her words seemed to hang in the air and Stanley looked really uncomfortable. I gave her my *He's scared of the water – remember!* eyes and they must have been very good because Murdy slapped her hand on her forehead and looked truly mortified. But then her mouth went completely out of control.

"Or we could do it your way, us in the boat, you on the jetty and not in the water. That's fine too. You don't have to go in the water if you don't want. And I know it's not because you're scared or anything like that. Even though it would be completely understandable if you were after what you saw. If you did see it that is…"

All these words just came tumbling out of her mouth. I waited for Stanley to go volcano-level angry at me for telling Murdy about things I shouldn't be telling her about, but he didn't. He just turned his back to us and said, "It's just this way is best, that's all. I'm the one with the camera phone."

I decided we should change the subject. "So, the

loch looks good tonight, extra mysterious and magical, don't you think? The perfect setting."

The sun was just dipping below the horizon and there was just a little bit of light left in the sky. The water was a deep grey, purply colour.

"It really does," Murdy agreed.

"There is nothing magical or mysterious about a lake," Stanley said.

I ignored him. "It's out there, somewhere – the real Loch Lochy Monster."

Stanley said, "It's not."

"Lurking in the depths maybe," Murdy said.

"There's no such thing as monsters," Stanley said.

"There will be soon," Murdy told him.

"And we've both seen it," I reminded him. "Isn't that right, Murdy?"

Murdy opened her mouth to answer but before she could, Stanley said, "Funny how only you two have seen it."

"And Mr Dog," I corrected. "He's great at sensing the monster."

"He doesn't seem to be sensing anything now,"

Stanley said, which was true because at that precise moment Mr Dog was busy sniffing what looked like an old sock which had washed up on the shore.

Stanley grabbed hold of the cart handle and began dragging it towards the end of the pier. "We can't wait here for a non-existent monster to turn up and save the day. Let's launch our own."

Once we'd helped get the monster into position, Murdy and I jumped into the boat and rowed round to meet it.

"I'll count down from three then I'll push it in," Stanley called. "Are you ready?"

I gave him the thumbs up. "Affirmative."

"Okay," Stanley began. "Three...two..."

"Wait!" I suddenly remembered we had forgotten something incredibly important.

"What now, Benji?"

"We need to say a quick prayer, just so we've got everybody who's anybody on our side."

"Is that really necessary?" Stanley said.

As if he had to ask! "Of course it's necessary, Stanley."

He put his hands on his hips and did a big sigh. "Fine but make it quick."

I closed my eyes and put my hands together. "Dear God and lords Vishnu and Brahma and the goddess Guanyin –" Murdy gave me a smile when I said that – "and Spider-Man and in actual fact any superheroes who may be able to offer their support during this venture. Please bless our Loch Lochy Monster with good fortune and luck—"

"Same thing," Murdy said.

"What?"

"Fortune and luck are the same thing."

"Don't interrupt him," Stanley said.

"Thank you, Stanley," I said, looking at Murdy pointedly.

"This rubbish takes long enough as it is," Stanley said and winked at her.

"Hey! It's not rubbish."

"Just get on with it," they both said.

I closed my eyes again. "Okay, where was I? Oh yes, bless our Loch Lochy Monster with fortune *and* good luck and make it look realistic and fearsome and very

Loch Lochy Monstery, so we can stop Gregor McGavin taking this place from Uncle Hamish. And from us. Amen and Awomen."

When I opened my eyes, both Stanley and Murdy were looking at with me with very sceptical expressions, but I wasn't bothered. I felt better now I had all our bases covered. Or at least, I thought I had all our bases covered. There were probably a few more requests I should have put into that prayer. Mainly based around buoyancy and plugs, but I didn't know that then.

CHAPTER 26

WHEN THE UNIMAGINABLE HAPPENED

It's funny how you can go from being so totally and completely positive that something is absolutely definitely going to work to realizing, in a matter of seconds, that it is actually going to be a complete and utter failure. If you'd asked me during our launch countdown how certain I was that our monster was going to be a huge success, I would have bet my own eyeballs that it would be.

Luckily, you didn't, so my eye sockets are still full of eyeball, which is good for me long term, but meant that I had to watch what happened to the Loch Lochy Monster model in its full devastating entirety.

We all counted down from eight, because Murdy said that eight was a lucky number in China and although we were in Scotland, I was never going to turn down extra good fortune. "Eight...seven...six... five...four...three...two...one," Murdy and I chanted from the boat very enthusiastically, and then Stanley pushed the monster's bathtub belly, and it dropped off the jetty into the water.

Mr Dog barked his approval and we all cheered when it landed with a truly impressive splash.

"Oh wow, oh wow!" I whooped. "It really does look monstery!"

Murdy let out a peal of laughter and thrust her oar skywards. "The Loch Lochy Monster lives!" And we all cheered some more.

But the cheering came to an abrupt stop when we heard three large spluttering gulps which sounded like they were coming from the monster's bathtub belly.

"What was that?" Murdy asked, lowering her oar.

"I don't know." I looked over to my brother. "Stanley?"

Stanley didn't answer, but I could tell he was worried,

because his face had sort of folded in on itself with concern.

Mr Dog growled when the monster's belly did one more giant *gurrrluurrppp* which was so loud, that for a tiny moment I thought the model might actually be coming to life. Which would have been exciting.

But the *gurrrluuurppp* wasn't the sound of our monster's awakening, it was the last of the air gushing through the plughole of the bathtub. The plughole that no one had thought to plug up with a plug. A tiny oversight that had a catastrophic effect.

I'd never tell Stanley it was all his fault but, as he was in charge, it blatantly was.

I reckon it must have taken about eight seconds for our Loch Lochy Monster to sink to the bottom of the loch. All that work – gone so quickly. It was shattering.

No one said anything for ages, we just looked at the spot where the Land-Rover-snorkel-monster-neck had disappeared and watched as the last of the monster's death ripples surfaced.

Murdy broke the silence first. "That was not *exactly* how I imagined that going."

"I had envisioned a slightly different outcome too," I admitted.

"We didn't even get to try out its paddling feet," Stanley said, glumly. "I spent ages working on those."

So there it was. All our hopes to save the McLaughlin family home were sitting at the bottom of the loch. Because we'd forgotten to plug up the monster's belly button.

"What now?" Murdy said, sitting down in the boat. "Do you think we could fish it back out?"

"Doubt it," Stanley said, peering over the end of the jetty. "It's a long way down and that thing was heavy."

Then he looked at me in a way that made me think

he really thought I might have an answer. "Benji, you're the ideas guy – you got anything?"

I should have been delighted that he'd asked me, that he'd called me "the ideas guy". But the truth was, I didn't have a single visionary idea left in my body. I was beginning to think that maybe I wasn't so visionary after all. If even Stanley's model hadn't worked, I really couldn't see how anything I could come up with would be any better.

It is possible that I may have been a little overdramatic, when I said in quite a waily voice, "I don't know, Stanley. It's all so hopeless! I can't think of anything. I've got nothing!"

Mr Dog rested his head in my lap and looked up at me with big, concerned eyes.

"You will, Benji. You'll come up with something," Stanley called back to me.

I sounded even wailier when I said, "But what if I can't?"

"Oh aye, that's the attitude." Murdy picked up one of the oars and handed it to me. "Didn't have you down as a quitter. Your brother's right. You'll figure out a way.

Now get rowing, noodle arms."

After we had moored the boat, Murdy cycled home before her mum realized she was missing and Stanley, Mr Dog and I snuck back into the house. Uncle Hamish was still asleep, snoring very loudly, the blue light of the TV illuminating his face. Stanley turned off the TV, put a blanket over Uncle Hamish and then we crept up the stairs to bed. I put on my jimmers and climbed straight in under my duvet.

"No prayers tonight?" Stanley said.

"Don't feel like it. Not sure anyone's listening anyway."

"Still," Stanley said, "worth a go?"

I pulled my duvet up under my chin and Mr Dog curled up on my feet. "I thought you thought all that stuff was nonsense."

"I do, but you don't."

"What's going on, Stanley? Why are you being nice about stuff?"

"I'm always nice."

I cough-spluttered. "Always? You couldn't stand Uncle Hamish when we first got here and now you're

264

building monsters for him and covering him in blankets."

Stanley switched off his bedside light, maybe to hide – I don't know. "I was wrong about Hamish. He's alright."

"Yeah, you said that already. But what changed your mind?"

"Oh, just something I heard him say – it doesn't matter." Stanley sighed. "I'm sorry my design didn't work."

"It was a great Loch Lochy Monster, Stanley. You don't need to be sorry."

"It's funny how a tiny thing like a plug can ruin everything. One small mistake and hours and hours of work...gone."

"You should have seen your face when it sank," I said and let out a little giggle.

Stanley laughed too. "I couldn't believe it was happening. What's Hamish going to say when we tell him his Land-Rover snorkel is at the bottom of the loch?"

"Perhaps maybe we don't?"

"I think you're right."

Neither of us spoke for a moment and I listened to Mr Dog's breathing, which was actually quite relaxing. After a couple of minutes I said, "Dad will find it funny when we tell him, don't you think?"

Stanley took a moment to answer. "It's exactly the sort of thing Dad would find funny. Mum probably would too, but she wouldn't show it."

"I miss them so much, Stan."

Stanley didn't say anything. I couldn't see his face because it was dark, but I heard his breathing getting faster. Then the words rushed out of him. Words he'd kept inside him for so long. "It was my fault, Benji. I didn't tie myself on properly."

To start with, I wasn't quite sure what he was talking about. "What do you mean?"

"Why they drowned – it was all my fault. The storm was so bad. The waves kept coming at us. Again, and again. It was relentless. They were so big. I couldn't see the top of them. They blacked out the entire sky. I didn't know water could be like that."

I closed my eyes and tried to imagine what it must have been like for my family on the boat in that terrifying storm. The fear they must have felt. "What happened, Stanley?"

He took a deep breath and continued. "A wave hit us hard. I lost my footing and, because I wasn't tied onto the boat, I fell overboard. The sea was so rough, Benji. I thought that was it. That I'd drown that day. I tried to keep my head above the water, but the waves were too strong, and I was just so scared, you know? I didn't know which way was up, which was down. There was so much water. It swirled around me, crashed onto me, picked me up and dropped me down. You'll think I sound stupid, but it was like the sea wanted me."

"I don't think you sound stupid. You must have been terrified."

"You know the worst thing? Above all the noise of the storm and the crashing waves, I could hear Mum screaming, calling out for me. I can still hear her now, at night, when I close my eyes or when I look out across the water."

I clenched my teeth together. I didn't want to hear but I had to listen. I had to know everything that had happened.

"I was drowning, Benji. My lungs burned. The sea sort of expanded in my chest and stole my breath. I thought it was the end. I really did. But Dad saved me. He jumped straight off the boat. Didn't hesitate. His hands grabbed me, and he didn't let go. He was so strong, Benji. He pulled me back towards the boat and we were almost there, we were so close, but then another wave hit. A massive one. I don't think Mum was able to keep the boat facing forward and the wave struck on one side. The boat lilted too far – she couldn't do anything. That's as much as I remember. I came round when the rescue team found me clinging to the hull."

Stanley paused and tried to swallow away his sobs. "So now you know the truth. It was all my fault. If I hadn't fallen in, Dad wouldn't have had to leave Mum on her own and the boat would never have capsized. It's my fault, Benji."

I tried to say, "It's not your fault, Stanley. It was just a terrible accident," but when I opened my mouth, the words wouldn't come. Instead, I lay there, with tears streaming down my face and anger and fear and all sorts of other emotions I would never be clever enough to name, swirling around my body. I stayed like that for ages, listening to Stanley crying into his pillow while I was pinned to my bed by my feelings. Big, dark feelings.

I had to do something, before the feelings got too strong. So I got out of bed and climbed into Stanley's and held his hand and hugged him.

Stanley sniffed a big snotty sniff, then whispered, "He's been looking for them."

"Who?"

"Uncle Hamish. He's spent all his money searching for Mum and Dad. Hired the best there is. I heard him talking on the phone the other night when I went to the loo. That's why he's in debt with Gregor McGavin."

My breath got caught in my chest and I forced myself to say, "Has he had any luck?"

Stanley squeezed my hand. "No, Benji. He hasn't. I'm sorry. It's just been such a long time."

My heart sank. I closed my eyes tight and pushed the bad thoughts deep down inside myself, somewhere I didn't have to look at them.

And in my head, I repeated *It doesn't mean they're dead. It doesn't mean they're dead,* until I finally fell asleep, still clinging onto Stanley and Stanley still clinging onto me.

CHAPTER 27

OUR NEW ANGLE

When I woke up the next morning, the sadness hit me hard in the chest, but I wasn't going to let it win. I did what I usually did and pretended it wasn't there. I crept out of bed to let Stanley get more sleep. Uncle Hamish was in the kitchen on his phone and, because I had fuzzy morning head, it took me a couple of moments to tune in and realize what he was talking about.

He took the Cookie Crumbles box down from the cupboard for me and put it on the side and mouthed good morning before turning back to his conversation. "I'm telling you, Clara. It has to be a threat. It has McGavin written all over it. Who else would pull the snorkel off my Land Rover? There's no other possible reason."

There was, of course, another possible reason but I didn't think this was the correct moment in time to confess what that was. I didn't look at Uncle Hamish in case I had the look of a snorkel vandal about me. I tried to act casual pouring my cereal into a bowl but I scattered it all over the worktop when he said, "I've got a right mind to head over there now and start pulling things off him. Like an arm or a leg."

I didn't think that Uncle Hamish storming over to Gregor McGavin's for a morning spot of limb removal was a great idea. Especially as Gregor had nothing to do with it. Luckily, I don't think Clara did either because Uncle Hamish then said, "I'm not going to do it... Yes, I promise... No, not even a finger."

The front door burst open at that point and Murdy stomped in, wearing my AWESOME T-shirt, munching the remains of an apple. Her dark hair was in two lopsided bunches, one tied back with a red scrunchie the other with her green one – a bit like she had a port and starboard side.

"Your wee lassie has just arrived," Uncle Hamish said. "I'll tell her...aye...I'll see you later. Aye, I'll try and look smart."

Murdy chucked her apple core in the bin, grabbed the Cookie Crumbles out of my hands and poured herself a bowl.

"Your ma says stay out of mischief," Uncle Hamish said, passing her the milk.

Murdy took a swig straight out of the carton and wiped her lips on the back of her arm. "I'm not a wee lassie, I'm a mighty battler! And as if I'd get up to mischief. I am highly offended at the suggestion."

Uncle Hamish held up his hands. "Okay, mighty battler, don't shoot the messenger. Right, you two, I'm off into town. No playing with any heavy machinery or sharp things or explosives."

"What? Where would we get explosives?"

"Just covering all eventualities," he said giving me a wink. "I'll see you two later. Hopefully with some good news."

"Visiting more banks?" I asked.

He ruffled my hair. "I've got a really good feeling.

273

Now where did I put my best shirt?"

After he'd left and Murdy had polished off most of the box of Cookie Crumbles, we decided to take Mr Dog for a walk.

"Do you want to ask your brother if he'd like to come?"

"He had a rough night. I think I'll let him sleep."

"Fair enough. Was he upset about his monster?"

He was. But not the monster she was talking about. I didn't want to go into details, so I said, "Yeah, something like that."

"Maybe we can try and have a brainstorm of what we are going to do about making a new one?"

"Sure," I said, although I thought there might be too many other things going on in my brain for it to be able to focus on a new visionary plan. But as we walked along the path towards Dad's tree, I realized how good it felt to be outside. Mum used to have this theory about being indoors. She said roofs were good at keeping the weather and burglars out, but sometimes they trapped your feelings in too. She said often things didn't seem so bad if you got yourself outside in nature. Until that moment, I thought Mum had been a bit unfair about roofs, but as I walked along the path with Murdy and Mr Dog in the sunshine next to the twinkling blue loch, it really did feel like some of my worries were able to escape out of my body and float off into the sky. I even started to think that it might be possible for me to be visionary again.

Murdy threw a stick, quite a long way as it happened, and Mr Dog bounded off down the path to fetch it, his big pink tongue lolling out of the side of his mouth. "Do you think we need to come up with a completely new idea? Maybe building our own monster is too much of a challenge. I think we can say we have not been that successful."

"It is beginning to look like that," I admitted. "We've only got a couple more weeks."

"Maybe we need a whole new angle, you know?"

"I think you're right about that, but what?"

Mr Dog ran back towards us, bringing the stick back to me this time. I was a little self-conscious about throwing it in front of Murdy and I did that thing where you try too hard and hold on too hard and I thwacked the stick into the floor, about three metres in front of me.

Murdy stared at me. She looked shocked and delighted all at once. "What was that? Tell me that's not how you throw!"

"Of course that's not how I throw!" Okay, sometimes it is how I throw. I had no idea how I was going to cope with caber tossing in Scottish PE lessons when I couldn't even throw a stick.

Mr Dog looked at me, looked at the stick, then looked at me again. I swear he shrugged in disappointment before he snaffled it up in his jaws. He brought it back to me with this look in his eyes which said, *Don't mess it up again.* I could style out one bad throw, but two was a different story. In my head I said a quick prayer to God, Brahma, Vishnu and the goddess Guanyin and Spider-Man to help me do a better job. One or all of them must have come through for me, as I managed a decent throw and the stick landed in the loch. It wasn't as long as Murdy's throw – but at least it wasn't shameful.

Mr Dog chased after it and did one of his terrific

dives into the water. As I watched him paddling about, inspiration hit. It was as though all the gods and superheroes had finally listened and gifted me with a truly exceptional idea. Although Murdy didn't exactly see it that way to start with.

"That's it!" I shouted.

Murdy raised a questioning eyebrow. "What's it?"

"I know our new angle!"

"You do?"

"Mr Dog can be the Loch Lochy Monster!"

Murdy looked from me to Mr Dog, then back to me again, clearly not completely on board with my vision. "Mr Dog doesn't look anything like a loch monster. He looks like a dog."

"Yes, and a very excellent dog too, but he won't once he's..." I paused to build up dramatic tension.

"Once he's what?" Murdy asked, with a little less enthusiasm than I would have liked.

"Once he's in a costume!"

Murdy didn't say anything for several long seconds. Then very slowly she said, "You want to put Mr Dog into a loch monster costume?"

"Obviously it's going to sound a bit daft if you say it like that."

"You think there's a way to say it without it sounding daft?"

"Sometimes, Murdy, the most visionary ideas sound a bit daft when you say them out loud for the first time. Think about what people must have thought when that guy had his pet rock idea."

"You've lost me."

"Dad told me about him. He sold rocks that he'd picked up off the ground and stuck goggly eyes on them. I bet people thought that was a rubbish idea. But he made millions."

"I'm confused. Rocks with goggly eyes?"

"Never mind. Look, I think this plan might actually work. I know I said that about the other two plans, but this one feels different." Mr Dog climbed out of the water and came and shook himself next to us both. "Who's a good Loch Lochy Monster?" I bent down next to him. "Go on, growl like a terrifying loch monster."

Mr Dog did not growl like a terrifying loch monster. Instead, he put his paws on my shoulders and licked my face. I looked up at Murdy. "We can work on the terror element later. So, what do you think?"

"You know –" Murdy said slowly – "and I can't believe I'm saying this, but it might just work...if the costume's good and we make use of camera angles and we make the photos blurry enough."

"Exactly my thinking."

"There's only one problem," she continued, "where are we going to get a loch monster costume for a dog?"

It was a teeny oversight in my plan, but a flaw nonetheless and it needed addressing. Luckily, my brain was in idea-making overdrive. "The internet!" I said. "You can buy anything on the internet."

That seemed to satisfy Murdy. "Let's go back and look on Uncle Hamish's computer right now. What do you think Stanley's going to think?"

"I think Stanley's going to feel like he was right when he called me the ideas man." I grabbed her arm. "Now, come on, let's go internet shopping for an aquatic monster costume for Mr Dog."

Now there's a sentence I didn't think I'd ever say.

We raced back to the house, Mr Dog weaving around

our legs, barking happily. I don't know if he knew what was going on, but he seemed very enthusiastic, and I suddenly felt certain Mr Dog would be the key to saving the holiday lets. Uncle Hamish was doing his absolute best to help us – he'd fought for us to live with him, and he'd spent all his money searching for Mum and Dad – I was determined to do my absolute best by him too.

CHAPTER 28

DRESSING MR DOG

When we got inside, we charged up the stairs to see Stanley to let him know about our excellent new idea. He was still in bed, just staring at the ceiling.

"We've got a new idea, Stanley."

He propped himself up on one arm. He had big dark circles under his eyes. "You have?"

"It's a bit *out there*," Murdy said. "But just think about the man with the goggly-eyed pet rocks and how well that worked out for him."

Stanley pulled a face and looked at me. "What's she talking about?"

"We're going to dress Mr Dog up to look like the

Loch Lochy Monster and use that as evidence to get tourists to come here and pay money so we can keep this place *and* maybe Uncle Hamish can keep searching for Mum and Dad too! We're going to get a costume from the internet." The words tumbled out of my mouth and while I waited for Stanley to respond, I tried to catch my breath.

Stanley looked at Mr Dog, then at me and then back at Mr Dog in the exact same way Murdy had done when I'd told her the idea.

"Rock guy made millions," Murdy said.

I don't know if that was what swayed him, but Stanley swung his feet out of bed and said, "I guess we don't know until we try."

I had NO idea there were so many fancy-dress costumes for dogs. Mr Dog could have been a lion, the Pope, a unicorn, a tarantula, a carrot, an armoured assault tank, a pirate and a cupcake and heaps of other things. But there was no costume for a loch monster. In fact, the only costumes that were at all aquatic-based were an orange-and-white clownfish (which was cute, not scary) and a very sparkly mermaid (and

I just couldn't do that to him).

I began to get the feeling that Mr Dog wasn't wild about our costume plan because every time we clicked on an image, he covered his eyes with his front paws. I knew he'd help us though. He's very loyal like that.

CANINE COSTUMES

We carried on scrolling through the pictures of dressed-up doggies, praying we'd find something suitable – well, I was praying – but it wasn't looking good. "I really thought you could buy anything on the internet."

"Go back!" Murdy shouted. "What about that one?"

"That one?" She had to be joking. "That's a Rudolph-the-Red-Nosed-Reindeer costume."

"That looks nothing like a loch monster," Stanley pointed out correctly.

Murdy rubbed her eyes. "Sorry, they're all blurring into one. I think we have to face facts. For some unknown reason, nobody has thought of making a loch-monster costume for a dog. Both the human race and the internet have let us down. Very disappointing."

I agreed. The internet was a let-down and very disappointing. I wasn't sure about ruling out the whole of the human race though, seemed a bit extreme.

We scanned back over the costumes. There really was nothing passable, but I wasn't about to drop the dog-costume thing.

"Just because no one else has thought to make a loch-monster costume for their pet pooch, doesn't mean it isn't still a visionary idea."

"What do you want to do?" Stanley asked.

"There's only one thing for it," I said decisively, because the mood required someone to be decisive.

Murdy stretched back in her chair. "Abandon the dog-costume idea?"

"No! We're going to have to make a costume ourselves."

"Make a loch-monster costume for Mr Dog... ourselves?" She didn't sound that sold on the idea.

"Yes, make it ourselves. How hard can it be?"

"Making things ourselves didn't work that well last time," Stanley pointed out.

"Making a costume is going to be way easier than making an actual monster. You don't even have to worry about paddly feet. Mr Dog has his own."

"That's true," Murdy said.

"If someone's managed to make a costume for a dog that looks like a piece of bacon, we can definitely make one that looks like a loch monster."

Uncle Hamish walked into the room with a very funny look on his face. I quickly switched off the PC monitor so he couldn't see what we were up to.

"What's going on in here? Did I hear someone mention a dog's bacon-costume?"

I must have panicked – no I definitely panicked – it's the only explanation for what came out of my mouth next, but I couldn't have Uncle Hamish catching wind of our plan.

"Er, we didn't say anything about a costume. You must have heard me say consume...because we were deciding whether a dog would..." I didn't want to say it, but I couldn't think of anything else, so I went for it, "taste like bacon..."

Uncle Hamish's mouth dropped open. Murdy looked at me like *I* was the monster, Stanley shook his head and poor Mr Dog's eyes got really wide, like he thought I was telling the truth when I would NEVER EVER eat dog.

"Er, sorry, what? You want to know if dog tastes like bacon?" Uncle Hamish said very slowly, as if he was having trouble processing what I'd said, which was understandable. "You know you can't eat dog, Benji?"

I swallowed and then I heard myself saying, "Yes, Uncle Hamish."

Poor Mr Dog whimpered. I bent down to reassure him by saying, "Don't worry, Mr Dog – I'd never ever eat you. Even if I was absolutely starving," which was the absolute honest truth.

When I stood back up, Uncle Hamish, Stanley and

Murdy were still looking at me rather strangely. I thought it would be best to act completely normal and move on from the conversation.

"Did you want something, Uncle Hamish?" I said, as innocently and brightly as I could.

He puffed air out of his cheeks, then ran his hand through his hair and it did that thing where it stuck up in all directions. "I was going to ask you kids if you wanted a snack, but now I'm worried about what you're going to ask for."

"We don't want dog, if that's what you're thinking!" I said, but I was a little peckish. "What about a Penguin?"

Murdy shouted, "A penguin! I don't want to eat dog or penguin!"

"Not a real penguin, the chocolate-biscuit type," I told her.

She calmed down then. "Oh, I see, aye, I'll take a Penguin."

Uncle Hamish ran his hand through his hair again and it stuck up in all new directions. "Reet, I'll go and get you both a Penguin – the biscuit type."

"How did it go at the bank?" I asked.

Uncle Hamish pursed his lips, went a bit grey round the edges and said, "Let's not talk about that now," which I took to mean that it hadn't gone very well.

After he had gone to get our snacks, I turned back to the others.

Stanley said, "Poor, Mr Dog. You're so weird, Benji."

Murdy said, "So, so weird."

Which I didn't think was understanding or appreciative. "Didn't hear either of you coming up with a better cover story."

They didn't have an answer for that, what with me being right and them being wrong. I didn't want to dwell though, we needed to get practical. "We need to think about what we can use to make a Loch-Lochy -Monster costume for Mr Dog. I'm thinking we need a green body-suit thing, flippers and some kind of hood to cover up his ears."

"A green body, flippers and some kind of hood?" Stanley said slowly.

"Yup." I didn't know why he sounded so doubtful. To me, it was the makings of a brilliant dog's loch-monster costume.

"I've got a green gymnastics leotard at home. We could use that for the body."

I said, "That sounds like a fantastic suggestion! Well done, Murdy," because it is always good to praise people when they come up with an idea.

She seemed rather pleased, and I think my encouragement motivated her brain to come up with more possibilities because she then said, "And I've got a green swimming hat he could wear so we can't see his ears."

"Murdy, you are on a roll! That is another excellent idea."

"Is it?" Stanley said, doubtfully.

"And if you want flippers, I've even got some old ones we can put on his feet," she continued.

"Murdy!" I said, "that's three fantastic suggestions. Really well done."

"Flippers – how are you going to get flippers to stay on Mr Dog's feet?" Stanley asked.

"Elastic bands," I said.

Stanley rolled his eyes. "Of course, why didn't I think of that?"

I wanted to say, *Because you are not as visionary as me*, but it wouldn't have done much for team spirit, so I said, "I'm sure you would have come up with it eventually," even though he probably wouldn't have.

After Murdy had taken Mr Dog's measurements, I made arrangements for the next day. "We'll meet at yours tomorrow morning, Murdy."

She liked that idea. "I'll get the costume together tonight and we can try it on Mr Dog then."

"I have a good feeling about this," I said to Stanley, after she'd left. "Do you have a good feeling?"

"I have some feelings about this, Benji. Good isn't my strongest one."

"Please don't put a downer on this, Stan. It's all we've got at the moment."

"I just want you to prepare yourself. Unimaginable as it is, Mr Dog posing as the Loch Lochy Monster might not be the answer we're looking for."

"I know that," I said, but really, I thought that there was no way the plan wasn't going to work. As Dad always says, perseverance and optimism are usually rewarded.

CHAPTER 29

THE RETURN OF THE LOCH LOCHY MONSTER

We arrived at Murdy's house just after seven o'clock the next morning. I practically skipped there I was so excited about our new improved plan, but standing in Murdy's front garden with Mr Dog dressed up in a green leotard, flippers and a swimming hat, it suddenly seemed very cruel to take photos of him looking so ridiculous.

"What do you think?" Murdy said, proudly.

Mr Dog tilted his head and whined. I had to agree. He did not look at all monstery. He looked like a dog in a swimming hat, flippers and a leotard.

I didn't want to sound unappreciative, but I doubted

Mr Dog in his current get-up would fool anyone into thinking he was a loch monster.

"So, come on, what *do* you think?" Murdy continued. "It took me ages to get the leotard to fit."

"Er…" What to say… The costume wasn't *quite* how I had envisioned it.

Stanley didn't comment. He just made lots of weird noises, like he was trying to stifle a laugh.

If things weren't looking grim enough, Kay McGavin and her cronies suddenly came hurtling round the corner on their roller skates. They screeched to a halt outside Murdy's gate.

Kay shrieked and pointed at Mr Dog. "Oh my God, Little Miss Liar-Pants! What have you done to that dog?"

"Yeah, Murdy, what have you done to your dog?" the twins said in unison.

Murdy put her hands on her hips. "It's not my dog." She jerked her head towards me. "It's his."

Kay stared me right in the eyeballs. "What did you do to your dog, weirdo?"

To be honest, I'd about had it with people calling me

weirdo, so I said, "That is none of your business, weirder-o." It probably didn't make much sense, but I think I'd made my point.

Kay wasn't done though, she said, "I already told you everything's my business. Seriously, what are you up to?"

Even though I didn't think she'd piece it together, I needed to put her off the monster scent, so I blurted out, "We've dressed him up as a...mermaid."

Mr Dog made a snarfly noise which sounded a bit like, "A *what*?"

"Yeah, I said. He's going to be in a commercial for... tuna."

"A mermaid dog? Advertising tuna! If you think that dog could sell anything, you're the actual weirder-o –" then she added another – "ro," just to outdo me.

Stanley stepped in at this point. "Oi, you! Nobody but me insults Mr Dog or calls my brother weirdo or a weirder-o-ro even. Now, why don't you three roll back to wherever you came from?"

"Soon, I'll be rollering to my new home beside Loch Lochy." Kay smiled a smug smile, then pirouetted on her skates and did a little curtsy. She really was very good. I almost clapped. "Come on, you two, let's leave these losers and liars to whatever weirdness they're up to."

"Forget about them," Murdy said as we watched them skate off. "Mum says she can't be a very happy person if she's so mean all the time."

"Still, we just can't let the McGavins get their hands on our home. They're awful. Kay never deserved to have you as a friend," I said.

Murdy actually blushed, then said, "They won't get their hands on anything, Benji – we've got an excellent plan."

"Yes," Stanley said, trying to sound positive when I could tell he wasn't. "An excellent plan."

We all turned to look at Mr Dog again, which must have made him feel a little self-conscious because he bent down and covered his face with his paws again.

To speak honestly, "excellent" at that moment in time seemed like a bit of a stretch.

"You have to remember," Murdy said, "that we'll paddle out to the middle of the loch and take the photos from a distance. We can blur them a bit. I'm sure it will be very convincing."

"They'd have to be *very* blurry," Stanley said.

"The blurriest," I said.

I think perhaps I wasn't quite positive enough, because Murdy flicked me on the forehead with her finger. "Benji – you're the one who says you need to have vision! Where's your vision now? This is going to work and then everyone at school will stop calling me a liar and Hamish will get to keep his home."

She was right. I shouldn't write off the costume or the plan before we'd even given it a go.

Murdy then took it upon herself to raise our team spirit. "Say, 'I think Mr Dog will make an excellent Loch Lochy Monster', Benji. You too, Stanley. I want to hear both of you say it."

We hesitated, but then she prodded us both in the chest with her bony finger. I looked at Stanley and he nodded, and we both said, "I think Mr Dog will make an excellent Loch Lochy Monster."

Mr Dog did another little whine, like he didn't one hundred per cent agree.

We all tilted our heads to the side and examined Mr Dog again. "It will look better in the photos," Murdy said, confidently.

We walked back to the loch with Mr Dog hidden under a blanket. Murdy was insistent about this in case anyone spotted him and said, "*Look, that dog is dressed up like the Loch Lochy Monster,*" and ruined our plan.

Neither Stanley nor I thought this was likely to happen, but we went along with it anyway, mainly because we didn't want Mr Dog to feel embarrassed about what we'd made him wear in public.

When we got to the place we had moored our boat, Murdy took charge. "Come on, get in, the Loch Lochy Monster is waiting."

Mr Dog jumped aboard and positioned himself at the front of the boat. He seemed very happy, with his tail wagging and his tongue hanging out, looking very unmonstery and possibly more doglike than usual, even in his costume.

Stanley must have been thinking the same thing because he said, "Don't worry, Benji. I'm sure he'll look more fearsome in the water."

"Do you want to come in the boat this time?" I asked gently.

Stanley looked out across the loch, then back at me. I could see the defeat in his eyes. "I'm sorry, Benji," he said quietly, "I just can't do it."

I squeezed his arm. "It's fine. Honestly. I understand. You stay on the jetty and get some good shots. You've got the most important job – after Mr Dog, that is."

Murdy pointed out towards the horizon. "Let's head out over there while there's nobody about."

Murdy and I climbed aboard and settled ourselves down in our seats. We each took an oar, and with a stirring, "Onwards!" from Murdy, we began to row. When we reached the spot we'd chosen, I said, "Okay, Mr Dog, get in and look terrifying for us."

Mr Dog didn't have to be asked twice. He did one of his very excellent dives, disappeared underwater for a second and then bobbed up to the surface looking very happy and not at all terrifying, like I had directed.

I gave Stanley the thumbs up to start taking photos. Mr Dog really did not get the whole **be terrifying** instruction, but he was trying his best, so I encouraged him by shouting a few more instructions. "That's it,

Mr Dog, now snarl – look as scary as you can. Work it, Mr Dog. Show me those teeth!!"

I turned to Murdy and saw she was looking at me very strangely. "What is it?"

"I was just thinking how great you are. Going to all this trouble for your uncle."

I hadn't been expecting *that* and I couldn't stop myself from blushing. "Anyone would do it."

"No, they wouldn't. Your parents would be very proud, you know – if they were still here."

It's strange how just a few words can have such a big effect and I know she was trying to be nice, but the sudden reminder of Mum and Dad caused a swell of sadness in me that I wasn't ready for. I suppose it was always there, just below the surface, ready to spill out.

I took a deep breath and turned my attention to Mr Dog, but my heart wasn't in it. "That's it, boy, try and growl."

"How do you think he's doing?" Murdy asked.

I was about to whisper to her that he wasn't doing brilliantly. That he looked like a very happy dog in a swimming hat and leotard and nothing like a dangerous and frightening loch monster, and that we should give up, but I didn't.

I didn't because Mr Dog's happy face had been replaced by a very worried-looking face, and he had begun to whimper.

"Is he okay?" Murdy asked. "Are you okay?"

"I'm not sure. Mr Dog, you okay, boy?"

Mr Dog's whimpers grew louder. His terrified eyes grew wider, and I knew...I just knew...

The Loch Lochy Monster was back.

"Mr Dog?" I said, in a very wibbly-wobbly voice.

I felt the crackle of impossibility in the air as the water around us and the sky above us seemed, in an instant, to darken.

Mr Dog looked at me with what I saw as panic in

his eyes and began to paddle his flippered feet very furiously towards us.

A large ripple rose up from under the boat and slowly spread out around us.

"It's back," I whispered.

"Is it?" Murdy asked, her eyes searching my face.

Another ripple.

"Yes."

The Loch Lochy Monster was rising up from the bottom and Mr Dog was in serious trouble.

I shouted over to Stanley, but from his position he couldn't see what was going on. He just waved.

Two more ripples.

I wanted to yell at Mr Dog to hurry up and paddle faster, but my throat made a weird gulping noise and a very strange low-sounding wail came out of my mouth instead. I took a breath and tried again. "Mr Dog! Swim back to me!"

But Mr Dog didn't respond. I turned to Murdy in desperation. "We need to get him out, Murdy, and quick!"

Murdy, her brow rumpled in concern, said, "We do?

Are you sure you're okay, Benji?"

Why was she waiting? "Yes, Murdy! Now! We need to get him out now!"

"Okay! If you say so!" Thankfully she got a bit more practical and shouted, "Hang on to this!" and she stretched out her oar for Mr Dog.

Mr Dog tried to get his paws round it, but his stupid flippers stopped him from grabbing hold.

"He can't grab it!" she said.

"You're going to have to swim for it, Mr Dog!" I shouted. "It's not far – doggy-paddle like you've never doggy-paddled before."

Mr Dog looked at me with desperation in his eyes. "Hurry up, Mr Dog! Paddle! It's coming! It's going to eat you!"

Mr Dog didn't hurry up. Instead, he stopped paddling altogether which did not seem like the best idea in the circumstances, but I think he must have become paralysed by fear. On reflection, my comment about getting eaten possibly wasn't the most helpful.

The boat juddered to one side, then the other. "Is it me?" I said. "Or are we moving backwards?"

Murdy stared at me. "Backwards? Are you sure? How could that be happening?"

I had no idea, but I did know that the distance between us and Mr Dog was getting bigger. I began paddling with my oar and shouted at Murdy to do the same. But no matter how hard we paddled, we didn't get any closer.

Three more ripples.

"Don't worry, Mr Dog! I won't let anything happen to you!" I shouted and I absolutely meant it.

CHAPTER 30

A BOY'S BEST FRIEND

Our boat came to a stop about thirty metres away from Mr Dog. We continued to thrash about with the oars to try and get to him, but no matter how hard we paddled, we didn't get any closer. It was as though we were anchored to the spot. I scanned the surface of the water trying to make out any monstery shapes. If it was close to us, it must have been right down in the depths.

"Don't worry, Mr Dog," I shouted as Mr Dog doggy-paddled in circles. "Hang on, boy. We'll think of something." I tried to sound confident, but what do you do when you're watching the best dog in the world about to get eaten by the very loch monster he is dressed up as?

It was a desperate situation. What Dad would call *a puzzler*.

Murdy grabbed my shoulders. "What's going on, Benji? Are you okay?"

"I'm okay, it's Mr Dog I'm worried about."

"Okay," Murdy said, slowly. "What do you want to do?"

I knew immediately there was only one thing I could do. I had to go into the water and save him. I tightened the straps on my life jacket and edged towards the front of the boat.

Murdy grabbed my arm. "Benji, no, there's—"

"I have to, Murdy, Mr Dog needs me."

And before she could say anything or I could change my mind, I glanced towards Stanley back on the shore, and then I jumped in. Just like my dad had when he saved my big brother.

I burst to the surface, arms flapping, and chest heaving and yelled to Murdy, "Shout if you see the monster."

She looked uncertain.

"Murdy! Keep a lookout!"

"Okay, of course." She held her oar aloft. "I'll batter it to death with my paddle if I see it."

I looked over to Mr Dog. I could just about see his green swimming cap – he was still a good thirty or so metres away. Poor Mr Dog, he looked exhausted and terrified. I had to save him. I swam faster than I have ever swum before. Probably faster than any kid has swum before. I suppose the thought of being monster food inspires surprising speed. I imagine I must have looked very heroic.

When I reached Mr Dog, he was very relieved to see me. I put his flippered paws round my neck and, without even pausing to catch my breath, I began to swim back towards Murdy. I wanted to get out of the monster-infested water and back into that boat quickly.

I was a bit slower on the return journey on account of Mr Dog hanging off me. I think his fur must have acted a bit like a sponge, because he was heavier than usual from all the extra water weight.

A little unhelpfully, Murdy shouted things like,

"Hurry up! I'm worried about you!" and "Swim faster!" as if I hadn't thought of doing that myself. What did she think I was going to do – some leisurely head-up breaststroke? No, I was frantically front-crawling as fast as my arms and legs would go.

I was about halfway back when I felt something thick and slippery brush past my leg. My whole body contracted from my knees upwards and, propelled by the terrible shock, I shot forward like a torpedo. Well, a torpedo with a dog strapped to its back.

I don't think I'd ever been so scared.

But then the waves started.

And my fear doubled.

I kicked harder and tried to say, *Hold on, Mr Dog*, but water sloshed up into my mouth and it sounded more like *huglubglubglub*. I felt his paws tighten round me, so I think he'd worked out what I meant.

The next wave that hit us was even bigger and it crashed down on our heads and gave my nostrils a very good cleaning out. Through the splashes, I could see Murdy was trying her best to paddle towards us, but she was struggling in the choppy waters.

"What's going on, Benji?" Murdy shouted at me. "Tell me how to help you!"

I tried to think, but it wasn't the ideal environment for me to be at my most visionary.

But, luckily, an idea hit me just as another wave did.

"*Huglubglubglub*," I shouted at Murdy.

She was not as good at deciphering mouth-full-of-water speak as Mr Dog because she just said, "*What?*" in a rather impatient tone.

"Throw the rope *huglubglubglub* – the mooring rope."

She understood that and scrambled across the boat, picked up the rope and chucked it. It was not a good throw.

"You need to throw it further *huglubglubglub* than that!"

"You think?"

Staggering around as the boat was tossed about on the waves, she eventually managed to pull the rope back in. She wound it up, swung it back and forth and then launched it again. This time, it landed only a few metres from us. I thrashed about until I was close enough to make a grab for the end. When I had hold of it, Murdy began to pull. It can't have been easy, but she pulled and she pulled and then, eventually, when we were only a few metres from the boat, the waves stopped. Just as suddenly as they had started.

"It's okay," I said. "I think it's gone."

Murdy stopped pulling. She looked around. Her face relaxed. "Are you okay, Benji? You scared me there for a moment. I didn't know what was going on."

I thought it was pretty obvious what was going on. I drew in a deep lungful of air and let it out slowly and scanned the water. There was no sign of anything monstery. We were safe. We'd made it. I felt Mr Dog's tight grip relax slightly.

But just as I began to take the last few strokes towards the boat, the monster appeared.

CHAPTER 31

THE DEPTHS OF LOCH LOCHY

"It's back," I shouted, stating the obvious. "The Loch Lochy Monster is back!"

Murdy, her face full of confusion, opened her mouth, in what I thought was a silent scream. I also opened my mouth in a silent scream and although I couldn't see Mr Dog's face, I was fairly certain he was doing the silent scream thing too. It really was one of those situations that called for a lot of silent screaming, because a large bit of monster (I'm not sure which bit – could have been a bit of back, or neck or elbow) had risen up in the water right between me, Mr Dog and the boat.

The large black muscular mass seemed to be pulsating. Throbbing. Beating. It rose up higher and higher as though it was trying to demonstrate its sheer size. The water around us grew colder. I felt Mr Dog trembling on my back and Murdy just started shouting, "Benji! Benji! What's going on?" like it wasn't completely obvious.

The monster made a noise like no noise I'd ever heard before. Low and mournful. It was more the sort of noise that you feel rather than hear. It seemed to pass straight through my body, right into the middle of my bones. Right where you store away things like love and sadness. And hope.

Then the water grew a little bit warmer, but that had less to do with the monster and more to do with me losing control of my bladder. What can I say? It was a very stressful moment and I had drunk an awful lot of loch water.

Just as I started frantically praying to God and the lords and Guanyin and Spider-Man and magpies and anything else I could think of, a crackle of blue light lit up the loch – a fork of lightning streaking through the dark blue. The hairs on my body prickled like static electricity. I looked at Murdy and saw that all her hair was standing on end, like she'd stuck her fingers in a plug socket. If I hadn't been so terrified, I would have laughed.

I waited for something to happen – for the monster to make its move. But it didn't. It just stayed there, between us. Existing.

For a moment, my fear was replaced by curiosity. I couldn't stop looking at it. I suppose it's not every day that you're that close to a genuine loch monster. Its skin was like nothing I had seen before. The blackest of blacks, but somehow shiny – reflective even. I could almost see my own face staring back at me. I wanted to reach out and touch the creature – to see what it felt like. Obviously I didn't, because you'd have to be a proper birdbrain to pet the Loch Lochy Monster, but despite my absolute terror, I was tempted. It was so black. So dark.

Because I'd been in a bit of a trance looking at the monster, I hadn't paid attention to what Murdy was

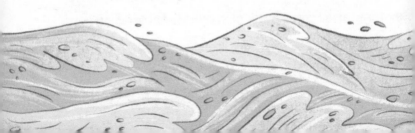

up to. She'd stopped saying *"W…w…what's going on!"* and had her oar raised above her head like she meant to wallop the monster with it. To me, annoying the loch monster by whacking it didn't seem like the best course of action, when Mr Dog and I were in the water so close to it. Before I could say anything, she brought the oar down with a massive whack and said, "Grab hold of this!"

The monster made a loud shrieking noise that pierced the air and Murdy let go of the oar. She hadn't annoyed the monster by hitting it, she'd angered it. It disappeared under the water in a torrent of angry bubbles.

"Where is it?" I shouted.

Murdy didn't get a chance to answer, but I knew by the terror in her eyes that it was right under me. It wanted me.

I pulled Mr Dog off my neck and pushed him towards the boat. "Swim, Mr Dog, swim!" I shouted just as something muscular wound round my leg.

Mr Dog stopped still in the water and looked at me.

"Go, Mr Dog. Save yourself!"

The thing around my leg found its way up to my waist. I tried to kick myself free but the more I struggled, the tighter it squeezed. The more I fought, the harder it clung on. And then, before I could draw a last breath, before I could take one last look at the sky, before I could check Mr Dog was safe, it pulled down hard and dragged me under.

Down

Down

Down

Deeper than I thought possible. Down where the light couldn't reach.

But then I thought about Stanley, watching it all happening from the shore. And I thought how he had clung on when he could have drowned. And I knew I had to cling on too. I kicked back, and I kicked back hard.

I fought against the monster. I fought with everything I had to free myself from it.

CHAPTER 32

MONSTERS AND HEROES

The truth about monsters is they're real.

They lie in wait, ready to drag you under if you don't face up to them. If you ignore their existence. If you pretend everything's okay, when it isn't. If you say you're not sad when, really, you are – they'll make it their business to get you.

You have to be brave to take on monsters. And being brave can be hard.

Stanley faced his monster that day in the loch. He dived into the water that he feared so much, and he saved me. He fought through the waves, dived down into the deep and he put his arms round me, and he

315

clung on, and he brought me back to the light.

When I came around, coughing and gasping for breath on the shores of Loch Lochy, I saw my family standing over me – Stanley, dripping wet, Uncle Hamish, face white with fear, and Murdy crying. But no Mr Dog.

"Mr Dog! Where's Mr Dog?" I tried to shout but my throat was sore. Probably from all the coughing and almost drowning.

Uncle Hamish said, "Oh, thank the heavens! Benji, you're okay."

I wasn't worried about me being okay, I was worried about Mr Dog. "Where's Mr Dog?"

"He's here," Murdy said. "And he's fine." And then she burst into tears, which she furiously rubbed away.

Mr Dog poked his bedraggled head between Murdy's legs, then pushed his way through. He bounded over to me and licked my face like I was the best thing he had ever tasted.

I buried my face into his fur. "Oh, Mr Dog! Am I glad to see you!"

Uncle Hamish said, in a slightly angry way, "You're

supposed to swim in the loch, Benji. Not drink it!" Then he dropped to his knees next to me and grabbed hold of my shoulders and pulled me into him. The warmth from his chest radiated into me. "My poor laddie. What happened out there? I saw Murdy and Stanley dragging you off the boat."

"I...I..." I was too exhausted to explain and, besides, I didn't know what to say.

"Don't talk now," Uncle Hamish said, squeezing me tighter. "There's an ambulance on its way. We can go through it all later, when you're feeling stronger."

I tried to speak again. "How did I...I mean...I don't understand...I was so far down..."

"Stanley saved you," Murdy said. "He dived down and brought you back from the bottom."

At the time, I didn't realize that she was right about that in so many ways.

I looked over at Stanley. He was standing a little further back, his wet hair stuck to his face, his hands in his pockets.

"You saved me? You went in the loch?"

He shrugged. "Of course."

"Thank you," I mouthed.

And he said, "You're my brother," like what he did was the most natural thing in the world.

I guess where there are monsters there will also be heroes.

And Stanley is mine.

Caitlin, the very professional but rather stern ambulance lady, said that only one person was allowed to travel with me in the ambulance, and certainly no dogs, so Stanley came with me and Uncle Hamish, Murdy and Mr Dog followed behind in the snorkel-less Land Rover.

While Caitlin was busy taking my stats – whatever they were, actually, I don't think she ever gave them back – I whispered to Stanley, "Did you see it – the monster? Did you get a photo?"

Stanley stared at me hard, then said, "What are you talking about?" which annoyed me because it should have been obvious what I was talking about.

"The Loch Lochy Monster – did you see it when you were down there with me? The real one?"

Stanley studied me hard as though he was trying to figure something out, then he looked at Caitlin and said, "Are you sure he's okay?"

Caitlin patted me on the arm and smiled. "Everything looks fine to me. He's a very lucky boy."

Stanley lowered his voice and tapped the side of his head. "But what about up here?"

"Oi! I can hear you. What do you mean *what about up here*?"

Gently, he put his hand on my shoulder. "Nothing, Benji. Nothing at all. Let's talk about it later, when you're feeling better, okay?"

"Did you get the pictures or not?"

"Later, Benji."

Later came that evening.

Even though Uncle Hamish said I must be absolutely fine, because I'd eaten a whole packet of Wagon Wheels and half a packet of Penguins, the hospital insisted I stay in a while, to keep an eye on me. And to help me make sense of things.

Uncle Hamish went to call Clara to tell her he would drop Murdy back as soon as visiting hours were over.

With him out of earshot, I took my chance to find out whether we had any decent footage of the Loch Lochy Monster. I might be in hospital, but I still had to stop the McGavins from taking our home.

"So, did you get anything? You must have got something, surely?"

Stanley and Murdy shot each other a look.

"You've got to be kidding? We've got *nothing*? It was right there, in the middle of the loch!"

"What was right there?" Stanley said.

"The Loch Lochy Monster! What do you think?"

Stanley took a step closer to the bed. "I know the doctors say you're okay physically, but in my expert opinion I think you might possibly be suffering from some kind of traumatic shock. I don't want to alarm you, but I think we should get them to give you another look over. I think there might be something wrong with you."

He probably was showing brotherly concern, but I couldn't see that at the time. "There's nothing wrong with me! Why are you avoiding my question? Did you get any good shots?"

Stanley flashed Murdy another look.

"Would you stop looking at each other like that. Just tell me what you got."

"I didn't see anything, Benji."

That was impossible. He must have been able to see from the jetty. "What? Why are you saying that? Murdy, tell him!"

Murdy wouldn't look me in the eye. "Show him, Stanley."

Stanley hesitated.

"Show me what?"

Stanley reached into his pocket and pulled out his phone. He opened up the photo album and handed it to me. I clicked on the video and Murdy put her hand on my shoulder. Then Stanley sat down next to me and said, "It's all going to be okay, Benji, I promise."

CHAPTER 33

FACING UP TO THE TRUTH

After I watched the video, I put the phone down on my bed, turned to Murdy and Stanley and said quite crossly, "What's that supposed to be, Stanley? That's just of me and Murdy running about on the boat and then me diving into the loch while Mr Dog is having a paddle!"

"I know."

"So when was this taken? This isn't today."

"It is."

"Don't be ridiculous! Where are the waves? The darkening sky? Where's the footage of the Loch Lochy Monster?"

Very quietly, Stanley said, "There isn't any."

My heart started beating hard in my chest. "I don't understand. Where's the monster? How did you miss it? It was right there!"

"I didn't miss it."

"Er, yes you did, because I definitely can't see a massive monster anywhere on your video." I could hear how angry I sounded, but I couldn't stop myself. "That was our chance to save our home, and you blew it. You completely blew it!"

Very gently, Murdy said, "No, he didn't."

I glared at her. "How can you say that?" I swallowed hard. "The monster was right there, and he didn't get a single shot!"

"He didn't blow it, Benji." Murdy paused and looked like she was gathering the courage to carry on. "He didn't blow it because the monster wasn't there."

I couldn't believe what I was hearing. "You're telling me the monster you walloped with an oar wasn't there?"

Murdy nodded and looked at the floor, almost like she was ashamed. "I didn't wallop anything; I was holding the oar out for you."

"How can you say that? *Why* are you saying that?"

"Because it's true." She closed her eyes and took a breath, then said, "There's no such thing as the Loch Lochy Monster. You made it all up. It was all in your head."

"What?"

"I played along the first time. I thought it was part of some kind of game." She was looking at me now, but I couldn't really see her. My head was swimming. I wanted her to stop speaking but she carried on. "I thought we were having fun," she said. "And then when you came up with the idea to make our own monster, I thought, if I had proof, Kay and everyone else would have to finally stop calling me a liar. But today…today was different. I could tell you weren't playing. You scared me. It was like you were somewhere else. Somewhere terrifying. And then you disappeared under the water, and you didn't come back up and I didn't know what to do."

I clutched hold of the sides of my bed. "You're making this up. Both of you are lying. You have to be."

Stanley put his hand on my shoulder. "We're not, Benji."

I knocked his hand away. "No, she *is* lying. She's known for it."

"I'm not lying about this, I promise. I lied before. Kay was right, she was right about everything. I never saw a monster – I guess I just wanted someone to see me. After my dad left, I felt so alone. And I was hurting, and nobody knew. So I lied. I lied so people would notice me. So Kay and the twins might be my friends again. But I'm not lying now. You have to believe me."

"But the first time, you saw the monster then? The first time we went out in the boat and we both fell in. You saw it then. You said you did."

"No, I never did. Not really." Murdy had tears in her eyes. "Honestly, I thought it was all a game. I didn't realize you really believed there was a monster. I'm so sorry, Benji. If I'd known..."

I turned away. I couldn't look at them. "I want you both to go."

Stanley said, "Benji, don't be like that. It's not like I didn't tell you a million times there's no such thing as monsters."

This time I shouted, "Go away! I don't want to look

at either of you. There was a monster. I saw it. I felt it. It almost killed me."

Murdy went to say something, but Stanley shook his head. "We'll leave you. You need some time. Watch the video again. If you look deep enough, you'll know what we're saying is true."

I didn't say anything.

But I already knew Stanley was right.

You can't hide from the truth once it's been shown to you.

The Loch Lochy Monster existed.

But only in my head.

CHAPTER 34

THE BIGGEST MONSTER OF ALL

I spent that night replaying everything over and over again. Trying to work out what was true and what wasn't. I went over every word Murdy had said. Looking back with clearer eyes, I realized she had never actually said she had seen it, not to me anyway. By morning, the anger I had felt towards her and Stanley had gone – replaced by a whole lot of other feelings, like sadness, and worry and shame.

I'd really thought it was only Stanley who'd been clinging on so hard to what had happened, but now I realized that I had too. I was finally ready to let go and reach out. To reach out and accept the help I knew

I needed. Stanley had been right that I should talk to somebody all along.

And that somebody arrived not long after I'd finished my breakfast of scrambled eggs and orange juice. She said her name was Shona and she had hands that reminded me of Mum's and ginger hair like candyfloss. She was a hospital psych-something. Her title didn't really matter, she told me, what mattered was that she was there to help me.

"Great," I said, but then I heard myself say, "can you give me a load of cash to save my uncle Hamish's home?"

She smiled and said, "I'm not here to offer you that kind of help." Which, even though I didn't *really* want that from her, was still a bit disappointing, but she explained that the NHS did not pay that well.

I liked Shona, but boy did she ask a lot of questions. She is probably one of the nosiest people I have ever met. Way nosier than Marvin my counsellor from before. She fished around in her hair and pulled out a pen that I hadn't even noticed she had stored in there. And then she wrote down everything I said on her clipboard.

First, she wrote down boring things like my age, date of birth, address, religion. She said the box wasn't big enough to include believer in God, lords Brahma and Vishnu, the goddess Guanyin *and* Spider-Man. She then wrote down my hobbies, what my favourite subject at school was, if I liked Uncle Hamish – obviously I told her I did, very much. What my room at his was like. What sort of food he gave me. I thought it best not to mention the Wagon-Wheel breakfasts.

She wrote down everything I said about Stanley. I was actually quite nice about him. I said he was one of the cleverest people I know. One of the bravest people I know. And that I really love him. But for balance, I also said he could be moody and that he had terrible breath in the morning – almost, but not quite, as bad as Mr Dog.

She also wrote down everything I said about my parents. She needed to get a new piece of paper because I had so much to say. It was good to be able to talk about them. *Really* talk about them.

And then she asked about the Loch Lochy Monster.

When she had finished scribbling down all I had to

tell her about that, she stuck her pen back in her hair and put her clipboard to one side.

Then, in a gentle voice, she explained that after a traumatic event, your brain can do funny things as a way of coping. She suggested that maybe because I'd kept all my grief over my parents bottled up inside, it had come out in another way.

"You mean it came out as the Loch Lochy Monster?"

She looked at me with her kind eyes and said, "What do you think?"

Would you believe it? Another question! At this point, I really thought Shona was doing a lot of asking and not much answering for someone who said she was there to help, but I didn't point it out. She was trying her best.

Instead, I said, "I was so sure it existed."

"Look at me, Benji."

I looked into her eyes and she looked into mine like she really wanted me to take on board what she was telling me. "Know that it's true that every one of us has their own monsters inside their head."

"But," I said quietly, "it seemed so real."

"It was real, to you. We all have fears and worries we keep locked away and, eventually, they come out. In all sorts of different ways."

"I bet not many people have them come out in the form of an aquatic loch monster."

"I suspect not. But I also suspect that there are not many people like you, Benji McLaughlin."

Not to sound big-headed again, but I think she was probably right about that. "It's still a bit embarrassing though."

She gave me a mock-stern frown. "It is no such thing. I can think of no greater monster to deal with than the monster of grief."

It was a bit over-poetic, but I understood what she meant. And in that moment, I finally saw my monster for what it really was. I even knew its name. My monster was Grief.

I stayed in the hospital a few more days so Shona could keep an eye on me and help me feel more stable. I wasn't completely sure what being more stable meant.

I suspect, not thinking a loch monster has dragged you to your death might be a start. She also sorted me out with a counsellor to carry on talking to once I was sent home.

When Uncle Hamish and Stanley came to see me, Uncle Hamish gave me a twelve-pack of Wagon Wheels, a message from Mr Dog informing me that he was missing me dreadfully and couldn't wait for me to come home, and finally a very tight hug.

Stanley brought me a bag of grapes. Then he sat on the end of my bed munching on them and said, jokingly, "See, I was right. There was something wrong with you. I thought it'd be your brain, but I didn't like to say it at the time."

Shona hit his knees with her clipboard and told him off for that. A lot. She said something along the lines of, "There's absolutely nothing wrong with his brain. It's been working overtime, that's all. Your brother obviously has a very powerful mind. An exceptional mind."

I may have added the exceptional bit, but most of that was word for word.

I said to Shona, "Some people have, in fact, said that my brain is quite visionary."

Stanley said, "I can't argue with that."

Uncle Hamish ruffled both our heads and said, "They don't make many like you, either of you!"

CHAPTER 35

AN UNBELIEVABLE JOURNEY HOME

The evening I was allowed home from hospital, there was one of those dramatic summer storms. Uncle Hamish picked me up in the Land Rover. Clara was in the front seat, and Stanley, Murdy and Mr Dog were waiting in the back. Mr Dog was almost as pleased to see me as I was to see him. When I opened the door, he launched himself at me and licked every single bit of my face.

Murdy didn't seem quite as pleased. In fact, she looked anxious. She hadn't been to see me after that first day in hospital. Stanley said it was because she felt so bad about everything. When I slid onto the bench next to her in the back of the Land Rover, she said, "Benji, I'm so sorry. I was wrong to lie like that."

I'd already forgiven her – I would have made the Loch Lochy Monster up all on my own – my powerful and visionary brain didn't need her encouragement. And as she sounded very close to tears, I said, "Yes, Murdy. You were very wrong to lie like that – I do not have noodly arms. And," I continued, "you were also wrong about being taller than me. But I don't recall any other lies, only misunderstandings."

She sort of laugh-cried and gave me a hug. Which surprised me, and her, I think, because a few seconds into it she quickly pushed me away. Which was fine by me.

The rain really lashed down as we drove along the road beside the loch. The Land Rover windy-woppers were working really hard to keep the windscreen clear. Uncle Hamish said, "I hope the puddles don't get too deep. I haven't fitted a new snorkel yet."

We weren't far from the house when the lightning started. It flashed down onto the black loch waters and lit them up.

"It does look magical and mysterious out there. Just the place a loch monster might live," I said.

Stanley said, "Don't start that again."

I was about to say, "I don't know what you're talking about," when Uncle Hamish suddenly shouted, "What in the heavens is *that*!"

"What, Hamish?" Clara asked. "Don't shout like that, you almost gave me a heart attack."

But Uncle Hamish didn't seem worried about giving her a heart attack, because he kept shouting. "*That* out there! Do you see it?" He stopped the Land Rover, so its headlights were pointed at the water. Then he got out of the car in the pouring rain and started off down the loch path. We all raced after him, trying to keep up with his giant strides.

By the time we reached him he was pointing at the middle of the loch.

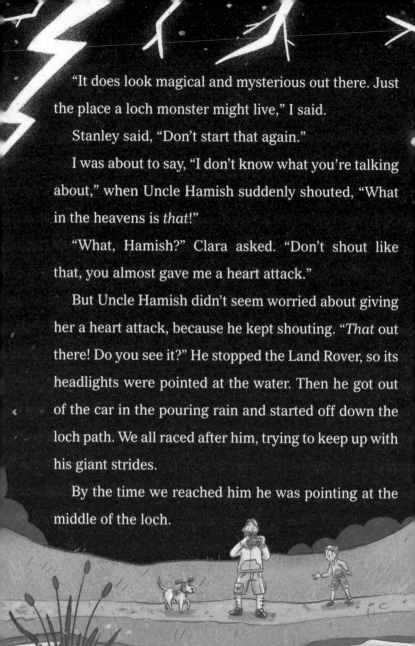

"What are you talking about?" Clara said. "Get back in the car, you're getting soaked."

"*That!*" he said, taking out his phone.

The lightning forked over the loch, momentarily lighting up the water again.

And we all saw it.

The Loch Lochy Monster.

Well, at least that's what Uncle Hamish and Clara seemed to think. Stanley, Murdy, Mr Dog and I all knew exactly what it was.

From a distance, and in the torrential rain, it certainly looked like a Loch Lochy Monster neck, but we all knew it was a Land-Rover snorkel.

We kept quiet, though, when Uncle Hamish put the images online. It was for a good cause after all – it was to save our home.

I guess, somehow, our monster had pulled itself up from the deep. Stanley thinks maybe the paddly feet hit a rock and kicked it into action. Maybe God, lords Brahma and Vishnu, the goddess Guanyin and Spider-Man finally got their act together and brought us some luck. I suppose it doesn't really matter because I was right in the end, at least about something. When people saw the pictures, they came in their hundreds to catch a glimpse of the Loch Lochy Monster. And with all the new bookings and media fees, the money came rolling in. We paid off Gregor McGavin with only days to spare.

Clara said Uncle Hamish should electronically transfer the money through to him, but he wouldn't hear of it. He said it would be far more satisfying to deliver a cheque in person. So we all drove round to the McGavin residence, a massive pile of a house a few minutes away.

Kay was rollering around their big front drive when we got out of the car. Clara, Murdy, Stanley, Mr Dog and I all stood back while Uncle Hamish stormed up to the front door and banged on it with his fist. When the door opened, Gregor took a step back in shock. I suppose Uncle Hamish can be quite an intimidating sight.

Uncle Hamish handed over his envelope and said, "Here's your money, McGavin."

To me, he looked like the BFG claiming back his own dreams.

Gregor opened it up and pulled out the cheque. He read it, put it in his back pocket and nodded sharply. He knew he was beaten. No way was he going to turn down twice what Uncle Hamish owed. Stanley thought it was very unfair and that we shouldn't pay double, but Uncle Hamish said he was willing to pay ten times that if he had to. Not that he'd let Gregor know.

Gregor McGavin said, "All seems to be in order." He closed his big front door and Uncle Hamish turned round. He must have looked about ten feet tall that day. It really is your character, not the length of your legs that lifts you up.

"Loch Lochy belongs to the McLaughlins. Always has. Always will," Uncle Hamish said, then winked at me and Stanley. "Isn't that right, boys?"

And we both said, "Aye, it is Uncle Hamish."

Then he said, "Thank the heavens for the Loch Lochy Monster!"

And Stanley whispered, "No, thank the heavens and God, and lords Brahma and Vishnu and the goddess Guanyin – even Spider-Man – for Benji."

As we drove away, Kay stopped roller-skating to wave at Murdy and Murdy gave her a little nod. In an unexpected turn of events, after all the media interest, Murdy had become a bit of a celebrity among the local kids. No one, including Kay, called her a liar ever again. Which was ironic – considering Murdy had actually progressed beyond lying to fraud – but I think, if your intentions are good, it's probably okay. Probably.

Sometimes, when I look out of my bedroom window and see the visitors queuing up on the jetty to go Loch Lochy Monster spotting, I wonder what it is about a monster that fascinates them so much.

Stanley says it's because people are stupid, but I don't agree with him about that.

I think maybe Shona's right. That everyone has their own monsters and maybe, by coming to see a real one, it might make them forget about the ones in their head. Even if just for a moment.

Or maybe it's because people like to believe in things that don't seem possible. Maybe it's all about hope.

Because even when there's nothing left, even after your grief has taken you to places so deep and dark, there's always a flicker of hope.

But something else I've learned recently is that hope changes.

It shifts. And that shift allows you to carry on living.

CHAPTER 36

HOPE

In the end it was me who told Uncle Hamish to call off the search.

It had been a year.

It was during those empty days after Christmas, when all the excitement of carol singing and turkey and wishing for the impossible present that didn't come had passed, that I understood that my parents wouldn't be coming back.

And while I still felt them, I knew it wasn't because they were somewhere waiting to be found. I felt them because they lived on in me. They were part of me. And they were part of Stanley and the love – the love we both had for them – would always be with us.

Murdy and Clara were at ours when I told Uncle Hamish. We were sat in front of the fire watching the BFG. I was using Mr Dog as a pillow and wearing my *Awesome* T-shirt, which Murdy had wrapped up and given me for Christmas.

Apparently, she thought it was a lovely gesture. Personally, I thought she was just giving me back what was already mine. I'd put it straight on, but I knew as soon as she'd given it to me, I'd give it straight back to her – once I'd pranced around in front of her in it for a bit.

I was halfway through my third pint of milk – I had been drinking the stuff religiously to make sure I stayed taller than Murdy – when I turned off the TV and said I had an announcement to make.

Stanley said, "Aww, Benji, but this is the good bit where Uncle Hamish starts whizzpopping!"

Murdy nudged me and said, "It's funny because Hamish looks a bit like the BFG," even though Stanley's joke didn't need explaining.

I blurted out, "Uncle Hamish, I think you need to stop the search for Mum and Dad."

Everyone fell absolutely silent.

Stanley sat upright in his armchair, blinking at me.

Mr Dog made a little whimpery noise – but I was sure. "It's time," I said.

Uncle Hamish came over, took both my hands in his and looked me right in the eyes and said, "Are you absolutely certain?"

I nodded. "I am."

And Uncle Hamish nodded back.

I had to focus on what I had and not what I'd lost. I looked around my home, at Clara and Murdy, Mr Dog, Uncle Hamish and my big brother, Stanley, and I was suddenly overcome with a lot of big powerful unnameable feelings and my chin started wobbling all over the place. I just had to get outside. Out from under the roof so I could let those emotions out. I turned to Stanley and said, "Will you walk with me?" I just needed to be with my brother.

Stanley didn't ask where or why or any other questions. He just said, "I'll grab a torch and our coats."

I didn't know where I was headed but I wasn't surprised when we found ourselves at Dad's tree.

"I've got to show you something," I said.

"Okay."

"It's up there. You'll have to climb."

Stanley smiled at me and said, "You know I love climbing trees."

I went first and edged myself along my sitting branch. Stanley put his torch in his mouth and pulled himself up to sit next to me, then stuck the torch between his legs so his face was illuminated.

"Wow," Stanley said, his voice completely full of wonder. "You're right, Benji. This place is magical."

I followed his gaze to the deep inky-black waters of the loch, which gently lapped against the shore below a sky studded with a gazillion stars.

"Would you look at all those stars, Benji. It's like Scotland stole them all!"

"Hey! That's my line!" I said.

We fell silent again, just taking in the enormity of it all. I understood what Uncle Hamish meant that first day here. The sky, the loch – life too, I suppose – they were all so huge. Monstrous and, at the same time, magnificent.

Stanley broke the silence. "Do you think Dad ever sat up here?"

"I know he did," I said, my voice breaking a little. "That's what I wanted to show you. I wanted to do it at the right time." I took the torch from his legs and shone it on our dad's name that was carved into the tree. "Look! You see that?"

I watched as Stanley took a deep breath, then, like I had done that first time, he reached out and traced his fingers round the letters which made our dad's name.

"He sat up here with Uncle Hamish," Stanley said. "He was here with his brother." He squeezed my hand, then he reached into his pocket and pulled out his penknife.

I watched in silence as he worked.

When he was done, he blew away the wood-dust then shone the torch on the trunk so I could see.

And there etched for ever in our dad's tree were our names, directly below his and Uncle Hamish's.

STANLEY AND BENJI
WOZ 'ERE TOO!

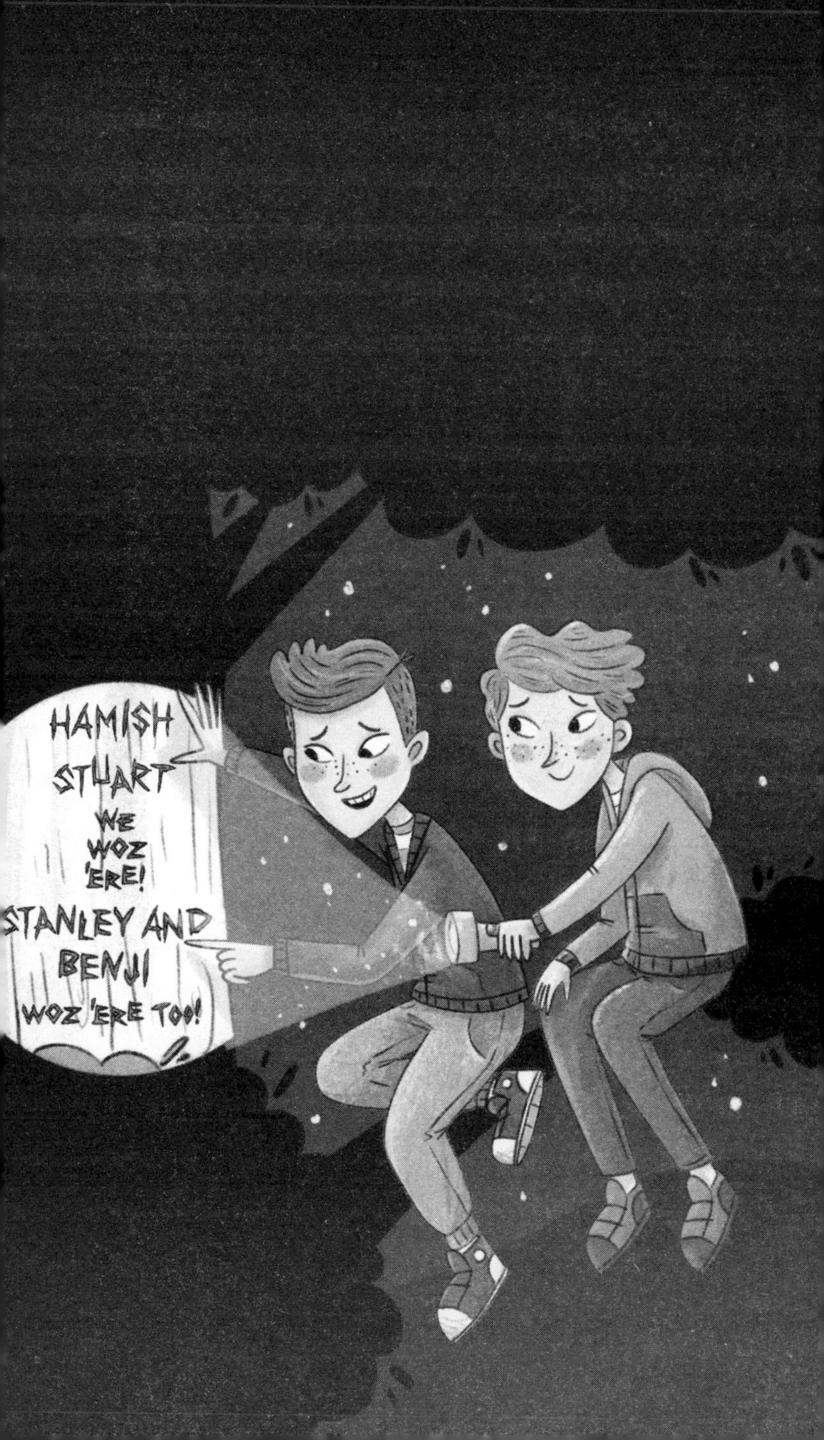
HAMISH
STUART
WE
WOZ
'ERE!
STANLEY AND
BENJI
WOZ 'ERE TOO!

And as I looked out over Loch Lochy, I felt it – hope still glowing within me. A different hope to before. For my hope hadn't gone when I'd accepted my parents weren't coming back. It had changed; it had shifted – but it was still my hope. I had so much of it, and I hoped for so many things. I hoped that Stanley and I would live lives that would make our parents proud. I hoped we'd always have amazing adventures together. I hoped that Loch Lochy would become so much part of us that its waters would flow through our veins too. And that our roots would always be there, as strong and everlasting as our tree's. I hoped that Murdy and Mr Dog would always be my friends and I hoped that Uncle Hamish would be happy and never find out what we'd done to his Land Rover snorkel. I hoped for everything.

I hoped for the future.

"I love this place," Stanley said.

"Me too."

"I think we're going to be happy here."

"Me too," I said.

And then, maybe because we were in an exceptionally visionary zone in that moment, or maybe because the

Loch Lochy Monster just wanted to show it knew how far we had come, we saw it.

A splash.

Right in the middle of the loch.

THE END

IF YOU HAVE BEEN AFFECTED BY THE ISSUES IN THIS BOOK, THE FOLLOWING ORGANIZATIONS CAN HELP.

Child Bereavement UK helps children and young people (up to age 25), parents, and families, to rebuild their lives when a child grieves or when a child dies. We also provide training to professionals, equipping them to provide the best possible care to bereaved families.
Helpline: 0800 02 888 40
helpline@childbereavementuk.org

Winston's Wish provides emotional and practical bereavement support to children, young people and those who care for them. Our expert teams offer one off and ongoing bereavement support and we also provide online resources, specialist publications and training for professionals.
Helpline: 08088 020 021
ask@winstonswish.org

PRAISE FOR JENNY PEARSON:

"Funny and touching storytelling." David Baddiel

"Hilarious and heartwarming." A.F. Steadman

"A gorgeous, heartwarming story full of hope, humour and love." Hannah Gold

"As funny and tender as it could ever be." Frank Cottrell-Boyce

"Jenny is one of the finest storytellers we have." Phil Earle

"No one writes humour and heart quite like Jenny Pearson." Katya Balen

"A big-hearted comic journey." David Solomons

"Heartwarming and genuinely funny." *The Times*

"Full of laugh-out-loud escapades." *The Sunday Times*

"One of the funniest books you'll read this year, with bundles of heart to boot." *The Bookseller*

"[A] heartbreaking and hilarious book." *Sunday Express*

"An action-packed and funny adventure story, written with lots of heart." *The Irish Independent*

"Pearson deals with tricky subjects with her customary blend of poignancy and humour."
The Mail on Sunday